# THE
# THREE
# COMPANIONS

**THE HARVESTERS Series also includes:**

**The Three Companions –**
*"The Land of the Palm Trees"*

**The Secret of Lilleshall Abbey**

**Bella**

**ISBN** 1 872547 71 0

Text © Richard W. Farrall 1993

Illustrations © Mary Lonsdale 1993

Published by Sherbourne Publications,
Sweeney Mountain, Oswestry,
Shropshire SY10 9EX, UK.

Typeset by Awelon Associates, Shrewsbury.

Printed by Clarkeprint Ltd., Waveney House,
45-47 Stour Street, Ladywood, Birmingham B18 7AJ

# THE THREE COMPANIONS

## PIGS MAY FLY

by

**RICHARD W. FARRALL**

Illustrated by Mary Lonsdale

Sherbourne Publications

1994

## CHAPTER ONE : AN ADVENTURE BEGINS

Nelly was bored. She wasn't unhappy, just bored. She had a good home, the people she lived with looked after her very well, in fact she had everything a goat could ask for. She would come in every night to sleep on a fresh bed of straw in her own stable and each morning the farmer's wife would take Nelly out into the orchard to tether her on a fresh piece of ground where she ate the fresh grass. Every day she would receive a bowl of corn to eat, along with tasty titbits from the kitchen, such as apple peelings, to which Nelly was very partial. No, she wasn't unhappy, nor was she depressed; on such a fine day who could be depressed. No, she was just bored.

"There must be more to life than this," she said to herself, and gazed out onto the rolling countryside, wondering what mysteries and adventures lay out there. She sighed, remembering a day not so long ago when a passing seagull had stopped in the orchard to rest; she recalled the tales he had told her about the sea many, many times bigger than the duck pond, and the ships that sailed on it travelling all over the world, and of distant lands where palm trees grew. It had sounded so grand and exciting that it made Nelly feel that her life was very dull and boring.

"If only......" she sighed despondently. At that moment a leaf from a nearby apple tree broke off and gently floated to the ground, landing only a few yards from where Nelly was sitting. Like most goats Nelly liked leaves, all kinds of leaves, but her favourites were apple leaves. Upon seeing the leaf land, she rose to her feet and made her way over to it. She had nearly reached the leaf when the rope by which she was tethered tightened, bringing her to an abrupt halt.

"Bother!" she said, and stamped her foot, very annoyed. She tried everything to reach the leaf; she stretched and pulled, even knelt down, but all to no avail: no matter what she did the leaf stayed a few inches out of reach.

"Just about sums up my day," she said, disheartened.

Suddenly she had an idea. If she were to back up and take a run at it, there was a good chance that she could stretch the rope just enough to enable her to grab the leaf. Well, it was worth a try. She backed up, counting her strides as she went.

"One, two three, er - um - what comes after three?" By now she was as far back in the opposite direction as she could go.

"Here we go!" she cried, and launched herself into a gallop. By the time she reached the other side she was travelling very fast, when suddenly 'Twang!' The rope broke, and Nelly found herself hurtling towards the apple tree. Unable to stop, she hit it head on, saw stars, bright lights, and finally a shower of apple leaves descending upon her, before she passed out.

How long she lay unconscious is hard to say but when she eventually woke up she had a terrible headache. Nelly slowly rose to her feet, wobbled a bit, and looked around, trying to remember what had happened. She was still in the orchard, which assured her that she hadn't died, unless Heaven had a striking resemblance to the orchard. No, she was definitely alive, her headache proved that. She then remembered the leaf and her attempts to reach it. But she couldn't understand how she had come to run into the tree: surely her collar and rope tether should have stopped her, so why hadn't they? She looked down, to see that the rope was lying broken on the floor. She quickly realised that in her attempt to reach the leaf, she had put too much strain on the tether and had broken it.

"Well, well," she muttered to herself, and pondered.

This fateful moment left Nelly with mixed feelings: true she was free, but......... She had been tethered outside all her adult life, and it was wonderful to browse the orchard unrestricted to eat what she liked, when she liked. Marvellous! On the other hand, she felt very guilty about breaking her tether, a fact that would not please the farmer's wife. Nelly was very confused. Freedom on the one hand, and the damage she had caused on the other, what to do? Nelly pondered her predicament, scratched an itch on her back with the tips of her horns, and decided that the first thing to do was to eat all the leaves she had knocked down.

"Much tidier," she thought to herself after she had eaten all the leaves, and returned to the subject of her new found freedom.

She gazed once more at the countryside and remembered the tales that the seagull had told her.

"This," she said to herself , "might be the only chance I will ever get to see the world, and I would so much like to see the sea! It shouldn't take long, I could be home before bedtime." And so it was, with a mixture of excitement and guilt that Nelly the goat jumped over the orchard gate and embarked on an adventure that would take her to many strange places, and to meet some even stranger characters.

\* \* \* \* \*

It was a lovely summer's day; birds were singing, the honeysuckle scented the hedgerows, and a warm gentle sun beat down on Nelly's back as she trotted down the road. She already felt very excited; she had never known any other world than the farmyard and the orchard, so even a walk down a country lane was a new experience for her. After a mile or so she came to a cross roads and with it came her first problem, which way to go? There was a signpost but, unfortunately, she could not read it owing to the fact that she had never learned how to read. She pondered there for some little time, wondering what to do, when she spotted a large grey horse standing in a nearby field.

"Perhaps he might know the way," she thought to herself, and made her way over to where the horse was standing.

"Excuse me, sir!" said Nelly, whose mother had always taught her to be polite when addressing strangers. The horse, who appeared to be dozing, failed to hear her. "Excuse me, sir!" repeated Nelly, much louder this time. The horse stirred.

"What is it? What's the matter? What's wrong?" muttered the horse, waking from his slumbers. At first he wasn't sure who, or what, had woken him up. But after a few moments his sleepy eyes focused on Nelly. "Who are you, and what do you want, waking me up like that?" he said irritably.

"I'm sorry to wake you, sir," apologised Nelly, "but I wonder if you could tell me which of these roads will take me to the sea?" The question seemed to puzzle the horse, who took a great deal of time before answering.

"You want to go to the s-e-e?" he replied deliberately.

"Oh yes!" enthused Nelly confidently.

"Why?"

"Because I want to look at it." This answer only seemed to confuse the horse further, who once more considered the question, before saying, "But you can't see the see; it's impossible."

"Oh yes you can. A seagull told me you could," protested Nelly.

By now the horse was getting really baffled, and was also beginning to think that the goat in front of him was completely mad.

"Look, little goat," he said sympathetically, "you can't look at something you can see... well you can, I suppose, but what I mean is ..... eh." The horse paused in mid-sentence, realising that he wasn't making much sense.

Now Nelly was beginning to question the horse's sanity. What Nelly hadn't realised was that this horse had

never heard of the sea, so the statement "I want to see the sea" was ridiculous to the horse. "I'm not explaining this very well, am I?" continued the horse, still trying to make his point. "You see, to see the see, it is impossible you see."

Nelly, who was by now convinced the horse was mad, started backing off, smiling and nodding at the horse as she went.

"Nor is it possible to look at the see. ...Hey, where are you going? I'm not finished yet!" bellowed the horse, as Nelly bolted down the lane, leaving behind a very confused horse. So Nelly's choice of which road to take was made more as a means of escape from what she believed to be a lunatic horse than anything else.

By midday the sun had risen high in the sky and it became very warm. The dusty road and the sun made Nelly feel very thirsty; she quickly came to realise that life on the open road had its drawbacks. At home there was always a bucket of fresh water at hand to drink from but now she had to find her own water. Fortunately it wasn't long before she heard the sound of running water, and a quick look over the roadside hedge revealed a fast flowing stream running alongside the road. Without further ado, she hopped over the first available gate she came to and made her way to the water's edge.

The water was so deliciously cool that Nelly considered it to be the best thing she had ever tasted. As she drank, she suddenly remembered something that the seagull had told her about the way all waterways made their way to the sea; the seagull didn't know why but said it was something all streams and watercourses did. Nelly quickly realised the importance of finding the stream, and that this was her best chance of finding the sea. Her problem was solved: all she had to do was to follow the stream and it would eventually take her to the sea.

Nelly followed the stream as it twisted this way and that, over large rocks, smooth stones, across stretches of open countryside and into dark little woods, but wherever it went Nelly followed. As she travelled she picked at the tasty plants that grew along its banks, the likes of which she had never tasted before. She met all manner of creatures as she went: water-rats, otters, kingfishers and herons, to mention only a few. It was all she had hoped for and more.

The hours flew by, as only they can when you are really enjoying yourself, and it wasn't until dusk began to fall that Nelly realised how long she had been travelling. She also realised that she would not be home before dark, as she had originally planned. This worried her, as by now her absence from the orchard would have been noticed.

"Oh dear," she thought to herself, "the farmer's wife

will be angry. Perhaps she's out there looking for me at this very moment."

The other thing that worried her was the prospect of spending the night outdoors; she had always slept indoors on her bed of straw, and the idea of having to sleep in the open worried her. She briefly considered going back but soon dismissed it, realising that she would never get home before dark. Her best bet would be to find a farm, or a barn, where she could spend the night in comfort.

On she travelled, always looking about in the hope that she might see somewhere suitable. As it grew darker, Nelly started to feel frightened: she'd heard stories of foxes and other strange animals that prowled around at night, not very nice animals that might attack a poor, lost, defenceless goat. In a nearby tree a large white Barn Own hooted and gave Nelly a start. By now she was really frightened.

"Oh what a stupid goat I am!" she wailed, "If only I'd stayed at home I would be fast asleep by now, safe in my nice warm stable, instead of being here".

She was about to cry when she saw a light in the distance; it was only a dot, but a light nevertheless. A light meant a house or some sort of building. It might be somewhere she could spend the night. Suddenly she heard a twig crack behind her; it was all that was needed to fill her body with fear. Without a moment's hesitation she ran as fast as she could towards the light, never daring to look back to see what might be following.

The light gradually grew bigger as she ran towards it, until Nelly could just make out the outlines of a farm. She galloped towards it, jumping all obstacles that came her way. Larger and larger the buildings grew as she got closer; she could not hear her imaginary pursuer, but was sure that it was only inches away. She leapt over the farm gate and flew into the yard, and headed straight for the stable where the light was shining. Without a moment's hesitation she jumped over the door into the stable. Once inside all she could do was pant with exhaustion, and tremble with fear.

Upon inspection, Nelly could see that the stable was quite large and the floor covered deep with straw; in one corner the straw was piled high. From beneath this pile, to Nelly's horror, came a voice.

"What's all this noise about?" it said in a rather booming manner. Slowly the straw began to move, becoming larger and larger.

"Oh dear," cried Nelly, "what terrible creature can this be?" She was so scared that she was frozen to the spot, and could not have moved even if she had wanted to.

The mound of straw shook itself, sending pieces of straw flying in all directions, revealing its occupant. It was a pig, and a very large pig at that. Now Nelly had seen pigs many times before, but never one like this: he was white, as most pigs are, but he was covered all over with black spots!

"Hello there!" said the pig in a jolly manner, and smiled broadly.

"Hello!" replied Nelly, relieved to see that the pig was of a friendly disposition. "I do apologise for dropping in like this but the fact is that I am ... was ... escaping from some terrible animal that was chasing me, and your stable was the first place of safety I came to ... so here I am."

"I see," said the pig, genuinely concerned. "Do you think it's still out there, do you?" he added hurriedly. One was hoping the other would volunteer to look, but neither did, so they didn't.

"My name is Nelly by the way," said Nelly, finally breaking the silence.

"Pleased to meet you, Nelly. I'm Gloucester," replied the pig, who paused for a moment before adding, "so what are you doing roaming about in the countryside so late at night?" Nelly told Gloucester all that had happened to her, and how she was on her way to the sea.

"Fascinating!" commented Gloucester, finding Nelly's

tale very interesting. "And do you intend to carry on with your journey?"

"Oh yes," replied Nelly confidently, who, in the safety of Gloucester's stable, was feeling her old self again.

"Good for you," congratulated Gloucester, "but tell me, where do you intend to spend the night, have you got somewhere?"

"Well..er...mm.. I'm afraid I haven't," admitted Nelly "got anywhere to stay ... that is, ..er..mm... not yet."

"You're more than welcome to stay here, if you like," Gloucester remarked cheerfully.

"May I?" squealed Nelly in delight. "That is very kind of you indeed."

"Certainly, make yourself at home."

Nelly quickly snuggled down in the warm straw. There was still one thing that bothered her: there had been a question she'd been aching to ask Gloucester since she had first set eyes on him. Finally, her curiosity got the better of her.

"Excuse me for asking," she began, trying to be as tactful as possible, "but are you ill?"

"Ill! No, why do you ask?" quizzed the pig.

"W-e-l-l..." continued Nelly awkwardly, "you seem to be covered in spots."

Gloucester roared with laughter, to such an extent that he was unable to answer Nelly's question for at least a minute. Finally, amid a lot of chuckles and titters he replied, "No, I'm not ill; never felt better! I've always had these spots; I was born with them: I'm a Gloucester Old Spot, hence the name 'Gloucester'."

By now the tears were running down his cheeks as he continued to laugh, leaving Nelly to feel a little foolish that she had not recognised what breed of pig her host was, but also relieved that her companion didn't have anything contagious.

They both made themselves comfortable in the straw

and prepared to settle down for the night. At least Nelly did. Gloucester on the other hand was doing a lot of thinking. Then, just as Nelly was about to drop off, Gloucester spoke.

"Look Nelly, I don't wish to upset you or anything, but I've been thinking about this trip of yours and, to be honest with you, I can't see you making it to the sea, not on your own."

"Oh!" was all Nelly could reply, more than a little hurt by the pig's remarks.

"No, not on your own," continued Gloucester, very positively. "Take tonight, for instance. What would you have done if you hadn't found my stable to hide in?" After considering the question, she had to admit to herself that what he had said was very true, but she certainly wasn't going to admit to it.

"No, what you need is a travelling companion," pointed out Gloucester, who could see that he had sown the seeds of doubt in her mind, "someone who, in a crisis, you could depend on. Someone brave, but intelligent, the sort of animal that no matter what, would not let you down."

"I agree," confirmed Nelly. "But where would we find such an animal?" Gloucester frowned.

"Good question," he added, grudgingly. After a few minutes silence, Gloucester jumped to his feet: "But of course, I know just the fellow!" he stated proudly. "The very animal who possesses all the qualities that we've listed."

"You do?" inquired Nelly, amazed that such an animal existed.

"Yes."

"Who?"

"Me, of course," he declared proudly. "It's obvious."

"It is?" replied Nelly, somewhat lost for words.

"Naturally, strange I didn't think of it before," remarked Gloucester, "but that's me all over: modest to the end."

"Is it?" was all Nelly could repeat, finding it all hard to take in.

"So that's settled then. We'll set out first thing in the morning," stated Gloucester. "Lucky you dropped in here tonight, bumping into me like this. You're a lucky goat to have me solve all your problems."

"Am I?" stammered Nelly.

"Oh yes, fate I suppose," considered Gloucester, "but whatever it was you'll be all right now, and think of the fun we'll have."

Nelly struggled to think of a reply, and by the time she had thought of something suitable to say, Gloucester was sound asleep, snoring, leaving Nelly somewhat bemused; but it had been a long day and she was very tired, too tired to think, and it wasn't long before she too was fast asleep.

# CHAPTER TWO : THE THREE COMPANIONS

Nelly and Gloucester awoke next morning to a glorious sunrise. Gloucester was certain that there was something he had to do before setting off, but after a few minutes of "umming" and "aarring" decided there wasn't. Nelly nimbly jumped out of the stable and unlocked the door with her horns, and the two friends were on their way.

They picked up the stream from where Nelly had made her escape the previous night, though Gloucester was in some doubt if there had been any danger in the first place; not that he would dare suggest it to Nelly, who was convinced that she had come within an inch of her life. They followed the stream in much the same way as Nelly had on the first day, stopping now and then to eat and rest, and it was on one such occasion that Gloucester confessed to his favourite food: acorns.

"Acorns," he said enthusiastically, "are without doubt the most mouthwatering, the sweetest, the most ... eh ... well words are hard to explain the flavour, the ... eh ... well they're simply the best things to eat in the whole world, and come Autumn all these oak trees will be laden with them." He gazed lovingly at the surrounding oaks which had first prompted him to impart all this information in the first place, before continuing, "And you and I, my friend, will spend many blissful hours just lying beneath them, waiting for nature's rich bounty to land in our laps."

Now Nelly had tried acorns before and, although pleasant enough, compared to apple leaves they were a poor relation. She was about to point out this fact to Gloucester when their attention was attracted to a disturbance in a nearby bramble bush. Nelly and Gloucester looked at each other, both wondering what it might be, and decided to investigate. As they drew nearer, the noise from the bush grew louder, and the bush itself shook violently. They paused, trying to decide what to do, whether to investigate further or simply turn around and ignore it, but seeing how neither wanted the other to see that they were afraid, it was agreed that they should both take a look.

"You go one side, and I'll go the other," suggested Nelly gingerly. Gloucester nodded approval. Slowly they made their way behind the bush.

"Of all the confounded, stupid, inconvenient places to leave a bush!" bellowed a voice deep from within the bush. Almost at the same time, both Nelly and Gloucester peered around the bush to see who the voice belonged to. It was a sheep, entangled in the briars, and by the way he was carrying on, was none too pleased about it. Upon seeing the two animals watching him, he stopped struggling and addressed his audience.

"Well, don't just stand there, get me out of this thing!" he shouted, obviously in a very bad mood. Nelly and Gloucester exchanged glances.

"I'm not helping him," declared Gloucester adamantly. "Those sharp thorns will cut me to ribbons."

"You're a lot of help!" wailed the sheep. "And what's your excuse?" he continued, looking accusingly at Nelly. This remark upset Nelly, who had always considered herself a generous soul, prepared to lend a hand to help anyone in trouble.

"Now look here," said Nelly sternly, "I don't know who you are or what you're doing in that bush but, if you want us to help you, I suggest you stop shouting at us and start acting in a civilised manner."

Gloucester was most impressed with the way Nelly was handling the situation.

"That's it, you tell him," urged Gloucester, fully supporting his friend. "Now let's get out of here and let him stew in his own juice."

"We can't do that," objected Nelly, appalled at Gloucester's suggestion.

"Can't we?" enquired Gloucester, disappointedly.

"Certainly not!" replied Nelly. "He may be a rude, loud character, but we can't just leave him in there."

"I suppose not," admitted Gloucester grudgingly.

"I should hope not," retorted the sheep, somewhat relieved. "Look, I'm sorry for losing my temper and shouting at you like that, but I've been stuck in this bush for ages."

"If you ask me, it sounds a stupid thing to do," commented Gloucester unkindly.

"Well, nobody's asking you!" roared the sheep, once more enraged.

"Look, this isn't getting us anywhere," said Nelly,

trying her best to take the heat out of the situation, even though she was herself a little puzzled as to how the sheep had come to land himself in such a predicament, and not for the first time in her life, allowed curiosity to get the better of her. "By the way, how did you manage to get stuck in there?"

The sheep groaned in dismay, and started to think that he was never going to be freed from the bush.

"It all happened," began the sheep wearily, "when I came down to the stream for a drink of water, and as I was on my way back to the field I noticed this here bush. You know how it is. I just fancied a leaf, and then another, and before I knew it I was in the middle of this rotten bush with the brambles tangled in my wool, stuck! Now will you please get me out of here."

"Very well," replied Nelly, who carefully made her way into the bramble bush to where the unfortunate sheep was imprisoned. Gloucester on the other hand chose not to join in the rescue mission, and remained a spectator.

"Why should I help that stupid sheep," he muttered to himself.

"What was that?" roared the sheep, unable to hear exactly what Gloucester had said.

"I was just commenting to myself that the stream looks deep," replied Gloucester cleverly.

"Oh!" grunted the sheep, half suspecting the pig's reply.

Untangling the sheep took Nelly quite some time. Each bramble had to be pulled out of the sheep's wool one at a time, amid a constant flow of complaints by the sheep; but finally after about fifteen minutes he was free.

"I think introductions are in order," said Nelly, after they picked their way out of the bush. "This is Gloucester, and I'm Nelly."

"Pleased to meet you," replied the sheep, shaking himself. "I'm Cuddles."

"Cuddles!" exclaimed Gloucester in amazement.

"Yes, Cuddles!" remonstrated the sheep. "It was a name my mother gave me because I was very cuddly as a lamb." Gloucester could not help but burst into laughter, and even Nelly thought it was rather funny that such a big rough sheep should have a name like 'Cuddles'. The sheep seeing, and not for the first time in his life, that his name was a source of some amusement, decided to change the subject. "So what brings you two out here?" he asked, totally ignoring Gloucester's hysterics.

"It's rather a long story," replied Nelly. "Why don't we sit down in the shade over there, and I'll tell you all about it?"

The three animals made themselves comfortable beneath a large oak tree and Nelly proceeded to tell Cuddles all about their adventure.

"And you really expect to find this sea then?" asked Cuddles, after Nelly had finished her story.

"Oh yes, the seagull told me about it. All we have to do is follow this stream and it will lead us there," explained Nelly.

"And he'd seen it, had he, this seagull?" enquired Cuddles, still a little sceptical.

"Well of course he'd seen it! He was a seagull," wailed Gloucester in despair. "Hasn't this sheep got a brain?" he added in a whisper.

"What was that?" demanded Cuddles, glaring at Gloucester.

"I said, do you think it's going to rain?" came the reply, which baffled Cuddles no end.

"Would you care to join us?" Nelly asked the sheep. "We'd love to have you along, wouldn't we Gloucester?" Gloucester groaned loudly at the suggestion, but before he could raise an objection, Cuddles butted in.

"Why not!" he declared, giving Gloucester a hard stare. So without further ado the three new companions set off in pursuit of the sea, even though Gloucester was none too happy about the new addition. Good progress was maintained that day, and they managed to cover many miles before dusk.

"We must find somewhere to spend the night," pointed out Nelly as evening drew in.

"I agree," yawned Gloucester, "I'm bushed." In fact he'd wanted to stop and rest for quite a while, but didn't want to be the first to suggest it.

"This seems a nice enough place, we'll stop here," commented Cuddles, looking around him.

"What, sleep out in the open!" exclaimed Gloucester, horrified. "The very thought of it! Sleeping outside might suit you all right but we're a bit more civilised than that. No, we must find a warm barn or a stable somewhere, full of fresh straw. There must be one locally."

"You want to sleep inside on a lovely night like this?" asked Cuddles in amazement, who had slept outside nearly all his life.

"It might be safer," added Nelly, remembering her experiences of the previous night.

"What's there to be afraid of? There's three of us," Cuddles pointed out.

"I didn't say I was afraid," declared Nelly, trying very hard to sound convincing.

"So why do you want to sleep indoors then?" reiterated Cuddles.

"Well for one thing, sleeping outside is common," replied Gloucester snobbishly.

"Are you calling me common?" demanded Cuddles, flying into another rage.

"No of course he wasn't," said Nelly, trying to avoid yet another argument. "Perhaps it might be fun to sleep under the stars for once. After all it is a lovely evening, and this is a pretty spot."

"Quite so!" agreed Cuddles triumphantly, pleased that he had won the argument over Gloucester.

"I suppose so," admitted the pig, grudgingly, "though I doubt whether I will sleep a wink out here on this hard ground, and I'll probably catch a chill or something. Not that anyone would care; but don't mind me, if I'm dead of exposure in the morning. I don't want either of you two to blame yourselves; it was my decision to spend the night out in this bleak, draughty ..."

"Oh do be quiet, Gloucester," interrupted Nelly, who had heard quite enough. They each picked a suitable spot to lie down, and settled down for the night. Despite his initial protests, Gloucester was the first to fall asleep, and snored loudly. Nelly, on the other hand, was still awake, worrying about the animals of the night.

"Cuddles, are you awake?" she asked timidly.

"Yes," replied the sheep. "What's wrong? Can't you sleep?"

"We are safe here, aren't we?"

"Of course we are," he assured her.

"There aren't any foxes around here then?"

"Oh one or two," came the reply, in a matter-of-fact manner.

"What!" screamed Nelly, jumping to her feet in fear.

"Oh, they're nothing to worry about," Cuddles assured her. "You shouldn't concern yourself with foxes; they're all cowards at heart, the lot of them. They wouldn't dream of bothering us. We're quite safe from foxes; they're not like ..."

"Not like what?" asked Nelly, who didn't like the way Cuddles had stopped talking in mid-sentence.

"Not like us, of course," replied Cuddles in a cheerful manner. He hated telling lies, but decided that perhaps there were things that for the moment should be left unsaid.

"Oh, that's all right then," said Nelly, feeling much safer in the knowledge that her fear of foxes was misplaced, and within a few minutes she too was fast asleep. Cuddles on the other hand slept lightly; a lifetime in the open countryside had taught him it was better to do so.

* * * * *

The next couple of days passed pleasantly, as the three travelling companions continued to follow the stream. It was a gentle, unhurried journey; they ate when they were hungry, drank from the stream, and rested whenever they felt tired. It was usually Gloucester who suggested the majority of the rest periods, but seeing how there seemed no need of any urgency, the others more than often agreed. They slept every night under the stars, a habit that both Nelly and Gloucester had come to enjoy, though Gloucester would never admit to it. They saw many wonderful sights on the way, and on one occasion, much to Gloucester's delight, they came upon a waterfall: he spent hours running in and out of the cascading water, squealing with joy as he did so. Both Nelly and Cuddles were convinced that he would still be there to this very day, had they not insisted that they continued their journey.

By the end of the third day, the sky turned from summer's blue to a dark, angry grey, and the sound of thunder could be heard rumbling in the distance.

"Storm's brewing," remarked Cuddles, knowledgeably looking towards the sky.

"It will rain before nightfall," Gloucester shivered as he felt the wind turn chilly. "I don't know about you two," he said, "but I would rather like to find somewhere to shelter before it does rain." Nelly was in full agreement, and although the rain never bothered Cuddles, he could see the others' point of view and agreed to find some sort of shelter before the storm broke.

"We passed a farm about a mile or so back," remembered Nelly. "Why don't we go back and see if we can find a stable or something?" All agreed, and they retraced their steps to the farm.

Darkness quickly closed in on them, and the first drops of rain were beginning to fall when they finally reached the farm. Luckily it didn't take long to find a suitable shelter for the night, a large barn that had been used for storing straw for the winter. No sooner had they settled themselves in than it began to rain.

How it rained! The tin roof over their heads clattered as the rain lashed down. A flash of lightning lit up the whole area, followed moments later by a deafening crash of thunder. Even Cuddles was glad to be indoors on such a night. From the shelter and safety of the barn, the three friends watched the storm unfold, like a giant firework display. Jagged forks of lightning flashed across the sky, and the thunder roared, while all the time the rain continued to pour down. After an hour or so the storm began to ease, and all that could be heard was a distant rumble of thunder, and occasional flashes of lightning far away, and the rain had subsided to a gentle shower.

"Well, that's that!" commented Cuddles.

"It's getting late," observed Nelly, looking into the darkness. "I wonder if it would be all right if we were to spend the night here?"

"I see no reason why not," remarked Cuddles, "as long as we're away early in the morning, before the owner of this barn wakes up. After all, we haven't asked for his permission to stay here, but I'm sure he wouldn't have any objections, so long as we leave it tidy before we go."

"There's some straw over in that corner: we could use it to make our beds," Gloucester pointed out, always observant when it came to the comforts in life. Each animal made himself a soft bed of straw, and it was not long before all three were fast asleep. It was still dark when Cuddles woke Nelly up.

"What's wrong?" she asked him sleepily.

"It's Gloucester, he's gone," Cuddles informed her.

"Gone?" questioned Nelly in amazement.

"Yes, gone," repeated Cuddles. "I woke up a few minutes ago. At first I couldn't make out what was wrong, then I realised I couldn't hear his confounded snoring … you know how he snores. Anyway, I got up and found his bed empty, and I can't find him anywhere."

"Have you looked outside?" asked Nelly, concerned.

"Only just through the door; but I thought I'd better wake you, in case you woke up and found both of us gone. There's no point in all of us wandering around in the dark looking for each other," explained Cuddles, logically.

"I think we'd better go and look for him. He might be in trouble," suggested Nelly. No sooner had they stepped outside than they heard a crash in the distance.

"Gloucester!" they both said together, and ran in the general direction of the noise.

By now the sky had cleared, and there was a full moon, and although it was the middle of the night, the moon was so bright that it could almost have been daytime. Perhaps it might have been better if it had been darker, because the sight that greeted the two animals when they finally located Gloucester made them both groan in dismay. Vegetable gardens are usually tidy places, as this had been, that is until Gloucester had found it. Never in their lives had either Nelly or Cuddles seen a picture of such utter devastation. The fact that the soil had been soaked only a few hours earlier didn't help, but the majority of the destruction had to be attributed to Gloucester. In places the garden resembled a ploughed field, where he had rooted up the soil; plant pots had been knocked over, marker pegs ripped from the ground: it was total chaos. Gloucester himself was finally located under a lot of bamboo sticks that had once been a frame for runner-beans.

"Hello, you two," he said cheerfully as he saw his two friends approaching, obviously very pleased with himself. "Look what I've found; bit of luck, what …? I woke up feeling very hungry, saw that you were fast asleep, so I had a look

27

around for something to eat," explained Gloucester meekly.

"Something to eat!" wailed Cuddles. "You couldn't have caused more damage if you'd driven a herd of cows through here."

"Oh dear!" said Gloucester, downcast, as he looked around at all the damage he'd caused.

"Oh dear! Is that all you can say?" fumed Cuddles. "This is private property you know. Someone had spent a lot of time and effort on this garden, only to have it wrecked by some passing, marauding, inconsiderate, oversized pig!"

"I'm very sorry," said Gloucester dejectedly.

"Being sorry is one thing," remarked Nelly, crossly, "but what's the farmer going to say when he sees all this mess? We could be in a lot of trouble."

"What's all this 'we' business," declared Cuddles. "It was him who caused all the damage, so he'll have to take all the blame."

"I'm very, very sorry," wailed Gloucester, amid a flood of tears.

"If he says he's sorry just one more time, I'll box his ears," threatened Cuddles.

"Well, I am sorry," blubbed Gloucester.

"Right, that's it!" and with that, Cuddles marched up to Gloucester.

In his rush to box Gloucester's ears, Cuddles did not notice a trowel that lay on the ground in front of him. Unfortunately it was resting on a stone, as a seesaw might, the result being that when he stood on one end, it catapulted into the air. All three watched with interest as it flew into the night sky, and then with horror as it sailed towards a greenhouse. The sound of breaking glass seemed very loud to all three of them, and had a stunning effect on all concerned. Before anyone could pass any sort of comment, a light in the farmhouse was switched on. They all froze as a man opened a window, and leaned out.

"What's going on out there?" they heard him shout. The man turned to address someone inside.

"Mary, where's my gun? There's someone in the vegetable garden. And while you're at it, 'phone for the police."

"Gun!" cried Nelly, horrified.

"Police!" wailed Cuddles, equally horrified.

"Let's get out of here!" suggested Gloucester, with which nobody was arguing, and they made a dash for it. All three of them raced out of the garden and back into the farmyard, heading for the gate and freedom; but as they turned the corner, they saw the farmer standing between them and the farm gate, blocking their escape route, and what was worse, he was armed with a shotgun!

"I want a word with you lot," he said, angrily, upon seeing the three animals. None of them felt inclined to talk to the farmer and promptly turned tail and ran. Unfortunately, the yard had only the one exit, which meant that they were trapped, a fact that quickly became apparent to them as they ran down one dead-end after another.

"What are we going to do?" asked Nelly, who was starting to panic.

"Hide. Anywhere," replied Cuddles, with a note of desperation creeping into his voice.

"In there," he nodded towards an open stable door.

The pair of them dashed into the stable and pressed themselves tight against the wall. Seconds seemed like hours; the waiting was unbearable as they listened for any noise that might indicate that the farmer was near. After a little while Nelly suddenly realised something.

"Cuddles," she whispered, trying to attract the sheep's attention.

"Yes," came the reply from the dark.

"Where's Gloucester?" she asked.

"Isn't he here?" questioned Cuddles. It was so dark in the stable that you couldn't see a thing.

"No," replied Nelly. "I don't think he came in with us." Cuddles muttered something that Nelly couldn't quite hear and, knowing Cuddles, she was rather glad she couldn't.

"He'll have to look out for himself," commented Cuddles eventually. "We've enough problems of our own at the moment." They both fell silent again, listening and waiting, until Nelly once again broke the silence.

"Cuddles."

"What is it now?"

"Can you hear something?"

"What kind of something?" asked Cuddles.

"A sort of creaking noise, in the loft above us."

Whether Cuddles had heard the noise or not, no-one will ever know, because just at that very moment the farmer switched on the light in the stable. As soon as Nelly's eyes had grown accustomed to the bright light, she could see the farmer standing in the doorway, pointing a gun in the direction of both herself and Cuddles.

"Got you!" he said, as he walked into the stable. "And don't think of trying anything: this gun is loaded!" Neither

Nelly nor Cuddles had the least intention of trying anything that might make their situation worse. "I've seen all the damage you've caused to my garden, you hooligans," continued the farmer, angrily, "and the police are on their way. You're in a lot of trouble. I've got a good mind to shoot you myself." The two animals could only stare at the enraged farmer in front of them, while he in turn stared at them down the barrel of his gun.

Suddenly there was a loud cracking sound and a splintering of timber as Gloucester came crashing through the loft floor above, landing directly on top of the farmer! As the dust settled, Nelly and Cuddles could see their troublesome companion sitting amid a lot of broken floor boards, with the farmer underneath him!

"That was a bit of luck," sighed Gloucester, rising from the wreckage. "I could have hurt myself, if he hadn't been there to break my fall."

The farmer remained motionless.

"Do you think he's all right?" asked Nelly, concerned.

"I'm fine," replied Gloucester, "but thanks for asking."

"Not you, idiot! The farmer!" roared Cuddles.

"He isn't moving," observed Nelly, who was becoming a little worried. Gloucester looked hard into the farmer's face.

"I think he's dead!" he finally pronounced.

"You don't have to be so cheerful about it," scolded Cuddles.

"I don't know why you're shouting at me! After all, he was going to shoot you," Gloucester pointed out.

"We don't know that for sure," reasoned Nelly.

"Well he was right about one thing: we're in a lot of trouble," remarked Cuddles. "Up to now we're guilty of trespass, destroying a valuable vegetable garden, breaking a loft floor, and murder. They'll probably lock us up and throw away the key."

"You forgot to mention the window in the greenhouse," reminded Gloucester.

"All right, and the greenhouse," conceded Cuddles.

"You really think that we could be in trouble then?" asked Gloucester, innocently. This time it was Nelly's turn to groan in dismay.

"Trouble!" cried Cuddles. "Trouble! You stupid pig! This is all your fault: if you hadn't wandered off in the middle of the night and wrecked that garden, none of this would have happened in the first place."

"That's just like you," roared Cuddles, angrily. "You wreak total havoc everywhere, even kill someone, and then try to blame it on someone else!"

"I'm not trying to blame anyone else," stated Gloucester. "All I'm saying is that I'M not totally to blame for this mess, as you would make out." Cuddles, although very annoyed with Gloucester, had to see his point, and for once was lost for words.

"Oh, do stop groaning, Nelly," he said, grumpily.

"It's not me who's groaning," replied Nelly, who didn't care for the way Cuddles had spoken to her.

"Nor me," added Gloucester.

"Well, someone's groaning," insisted Cuddles, who then paused to think, before adding in a less aggressive tone "and if it isn't any of us ... it must be ..." They all looked at each other, and as if in one voice, they all said, "The farmer!"

They all dashed over to where the farmer was lying: indeed it was the farmer who was groaning, and was also showing signs of movement.

"He's alive!" shrieked Nelly, greatly relieved. "Thank heavens!"

"And you said he was dead," accused Cuddles, looking hard at Gloucester.

"Well, he certainly looked dead," replied the pig.

The farmer slowly sat up, and rubbed his head.

"What on earth?" he mumbled to himself. Upon looking up, he saw the three animals looking down at him. "You lot!" he roared, "I remember now! Where's my gun?"

"I think now might be a good time for us to take our leave," suggested Gloucester, walking backwards towards the door. For once they all agreed with him.

"Run!" shouted Cuddles. They ran out of the yard, down a lane, through a gate, and across a meadow. In fact, they didn't stop running until they were certain no-one was following. They finally stopped, though collapsed might be a better description, in a small wood...somewhere .

After a few minutes to get their breath back, they discussed the night's events, with both Nelly and Cuddles reprimanding Gloucester for his stupid behaviour, making him solemnly promise that he would never do anything like it again.

"Just one thing puzzles me," questioned Nelly, turning to Gloucester. "What were you doing in that loft in the first place, and how on earth did you get up there?"

"Oh that's an easy question to answer," replied Gloucester, in a matter-of-fact manner. "I first discovered it when I was looking for something to eat. I thought there might be some potatoes stored up there, or something, but there wasn't, and when the farmer started to chase us, it seemed as good a place as any to hide. How was I to know the floor was rotten!"

"Yes, but how did you get up there?" repeated Nelly.

Gloucester smiled, determined to make the most of the mystery before revealing all.

"Perhaps you didn't notice," he finally said, "but there was a flight of sandstone steps on the outside of the building leading to the loft. It was as simple as walking upstairs."

"You know, I've just realised something," chuckled Cuddles, who then burst into laughter. "If Gloucester had killed that farmer, could you imagine the headlines in the newspapers - Man Killed by Flying Pig!" At which they all laughed.

CHAPTER THREE : THE RIVER

Fortunately, it didn't take long for the three companions to relocate the stream next morning. It bore little resemblance to the stream that they had left the previous night, having swollen with all the rain that had fallen during the night, and its waters were a muddy brown. Pieces of wood, broken branches, and even an old tyre were being carried along in its fast flowing waters. Once again they dutifully followed its trail.

By mid-morning they approached the gentle slopes of a valley where the stream appeared to run faster than at any time before, as if it were in a hurry to reach an important destination. Moments later the three animals found themselves gazing upon a much larger body of water that, even at a distance, appeared to be much larger than the stream.

"Is that it? The sea?" asked Cuddles, as they stood and stared at its silvery waters.

"I don't know," admitted Nelly uncertainly. "It could be." They continued to follow the stream as it raced joyfully to join the great mass of water. They stood in awe upon its banks. None of them had seen so much water in one place and, in Gloucester's opinion, the bank opposite was at least a mile away, though Cuddles thought fifty yards might be a more accurate description: but whatever, it was very wide. The water seemed to move slower than that of the stream, but was far deeper and it flowed off into the distance as far as the eye could see. Both Cuddles and Gloucester were very impressed by it all, but not Nelly.

"I thought it might be bigger," she said finally, with a hint of disappointment in her voice.

"How big do you want it?" asked Gloucester, amazed at Nelly's reaction.

"It looks pretty big to me," commented Cuddles thoughtfully.

"The seagull said it was huge," added Nelly. "I admit this is big, but it isn't huge." The other two, seeing how disappointed their friend was, tried their best to cheer her up.

"Look," said Gloucester, "there are those who exaggerate, you know: make out something is better than it is, boastful like. I had a cousin once who stayed with me; to listen to him you'd think he lived in a palace with all his grand tales, but when I saw his home it was a drab little place. This seagull of yours was probably a bit like him, boasting about the sea, telling you how big and grand it was, knowing all the time that you would probably never go there yourself to see what it was really like."

"He's quite right," added Cuddles. "There are some fibbers about. It's not nice to tell lies, but sadly there are those who do. But look on the bright side; you wanted to go to the sea, here you are! There aren't many animals who set out on an adventure like you have, and reach their goal. After all, it's quite impressive you know; I've never seen anything like it."

"I suppose so," replied Nelly, still far from happy. "But you know......"

"Tell you what, we'll ask someone where we are exactly," suggested Cuddles, who could see that they hadn't managed to convince their troubled friend.

"He will know," said Gloucester.

"Who?" asked Cuddles.

"That otter, sunbathing, over there," Gloucester nodded in the direction where he had seen the otter. "He's bound to know where we are." They all went over to the otter and asked him whether they had actually reached the sea.

"The sea!" he exclaimed, amazed at their ignorance. "Good heavens, no. This is the river, but it does run into the sea."

"Really," enthused Nelly, feeling much happier.

"Oh yes," continued the otter. "If you were to follow the

river, it would take you there eventually."

"Have you ever been there?" asked Gloucester.

"A couple of times," came the reply.

"What's it like?" demanded Cuddles, who had up until now always questioned the existence of such a place, but now he had actually met someone who had been there, was full of enthusiasm.

"Oh! It's a marvellous place," began the otter cheerfully "full of all kinds of fish, with huge waves that rise and fall, crashing onto the beach, which are just super to play in; and there are sandy beaches, and dunes, and strange little creatures that crawl in and out of the sea, and ..."

"Is it big?" butted in Nelly, who had forgotten her manners in all the excitement.

"Big!" exclaimed the otter. "Let me see, how can I describe it. You see this river here," they all nodded, "well, this river is to the sea as a raindrop is to the river."

"Gosh!" gasped Gloucester in amazement.

"That's big," commented Cuddles.

"So the seagull was telling the truth after all," said Nelly, who was becoming even more excited.

"Seagulls," remarked the otter, picking up on what Nelly had said, "there are thousands of seagulls there."

"How far is it?" asked Cuddles, getting back to relevant details.

"A long way," the otter informed them. "Many miles. A journey to the sea can take weeks, even months on foot as you are." Upon hearing this Nelly's heart sank, all her hopes and dreams dashed in a single moment.

"We'll never make it," said Cuddles bitterly, before turning to the otter to confirm what he had said. "Months?"

"Yes on foot," repeated the otter. "But why don't you go on the river. It will be a lot quicker."

"River travel might be all right for you," pointed out Cuddles.

"You've lived all your life in or on the water, but we are

land animals. We know nothing of the river, or its ways. I can swim a bit, I learned in a sheep dip, and I know Gloucester can swim, all pigs can, but not enough to swim all the way to the sea."

"I can't swim at all," interrupted Nelly, who by now was feeling very depressed.

"Well there you are," confirmed Cuddles. "There is no way that we can swim there, like you otter. It's out of the question."

"I never suggested you swam all the way," explained the otter. "I was thinking more of floating down the river."

"Floating? How?" demanded Gloucester, who thought the suggestion was one of the most stupid ideas he'd ever heard.

"On a raft," replied the otter.

"But we haven't got a raft," Gloucester quickly pointed out.

"I know that, but there's one stuck in that reed bed over there." The otter nodded towards the reed bed before continuing, "It floated down last night, probably broke its moorings during the storm, from somewhere up-river and got tangled in the reeds. It's been there all morning and as of yet nobody's claimed it, so I reckon you've got as much right to it as anyone. It's just what you need. You'll be at the sea in half the time it would take on foot, and a lot less strenuous."

The three companions discussed the otter's proposal, and despite a few reservations by Nelly, they all agreed to continue their journey by raft.

"Just one problem, as I see it," started Cuddles, after the conference was finished. "How do we get the raft out of the reeds?"

"Easy," assured the otter. "There is a rope attached to it. I'll just swim over, get the other end and bring it back to you. Between you, you should be able to pull it free." The otter dived into the river and swam swiftly to the raft, then returned to the river bank, with the rope in his teeth. Sure enough, after a couple of tugs, the raft was clear of the reeds, and within a few seconds safely secured.

The raft itself was a sturdy craft, consisting of four empty oil drums, a lot of good timber, with a solid deck made of planks of wood, surrounded by tyres, all of which was held together with strong rope. It even had a crude but efficient rudder at the rear of the craft, by which to steer it, operated by a tiller. The raft seemed in perfect condition, and the otter kindly swam underneath it to check all was well below the water-line, which it was. All in all the three animals were delighted with their new craft.

"What a marvellous idea this is!" enthused Gloucester, as he walked up and down the deck. "Just think of it, lazing about all day while the river carries us gently on our way."

"Well, there's a bit more to it than that, but you've got the general idea," said the otter.

"Any advice you can give us?" Nelly asked the otter. "We'd be very grateful for any help."

Trying to impart a lifetime's experience on the river to three complete novices was almost impossible, but the otter did his best, concentrating on the more important aspects of river travel, such as, always travel in the middle of the river, where it is deepest with less chance of running onto a sand bank, or hitting a rock; never travel at night, when they can't see, they might easily hit a tree or some other floating debris, and numerous other tips. The only problem that remained was the question of who was going to take the tiller. This turned out to be a major stumbling block, as both Cuddles and Gloucester thought that they were far more competent than the other to perform such a duty. The problem was finally resolved, but after a lot of arguing, by Nelly, who suggested that they should all take turns at steering the raft, that a rota be worked alphabetically, and seeing how 'C' for Cuddles came before 'G' for Gloucester, it should be Cuddles to take the tiller first. This delighted

Cuddles no end, who, for the first time in his life, was actually pleased with the name he had been christened with.

So, without further delay, they boarded the raft, with Cuddles proudly at the tiller, Nelly standing nervously in the centre of the raft, and Gloucester at the front, sulking, they began their river journey. For the first mile or so the otter kept them company, giving advice as they went.

"Why don't you come with us?" suggested Nelly, who liked the idea of having an experienced river traveller along with them.

"Love to, but I'm afraid I can't. I've got business up river." He swam a little further with them, but once he was sure that they had got the hang of steering the raft, bade them good-luck, and goodbye. The three animals thanked him for all his kindness and help, and said farewell.

Despite her initial fears, Nelly quickly found that she enjoyed travelling on the river, as the raft floated gently on. As it did so, the river itself revealed a world hitherto unknown to them. They met all kinds of animals and birds that inhabited either its waters or banks: graceful swans that glided effortlessly on the water; busy ducks forever dipping their heads into the river as they fed; long-legged herons that angled for frogs and newts in the shallows; brilliant coloured kingfishers, shy little moorhens, salmon that leapt, dragonflies that danced; water-rats, voles, shrews, and many, many more. It seemed that no matter how much they saw, there was always something new for them to marvel at just around the next corner, a treasure trove of nature opened up to them.

\* \* \* \* \*

The days that passed on the river were some of the most peaceful the three animals had ever known but, as so often in life there is always something, the unexpected, the unforeseen, waiting just around the corner, ready to turn the most peaceful situation into total chaos. It was almost noon one sunny day when the tranquillity was shattered. Gloucester was steering the raft, while Nelly and Cuddles were taking a nap, when all of a sudden, Cuddles rose to his feet, cocked his head to one side, and stared hard into the distance.

"What is it?" asked Nelly idly. "What's wrong?"

"I thought I heard something," replied Cuddles slowly, concentrating hard on something in the distance. "It sounded like ... Quick Gloucester, make for the bank!" His tone had now changed to one of urgency.

"Why?" asked Gloucester, somewhat bewildered.

"Don't argue, just do it!" ordered Cuddles with great authority. Gloucester did as he was asked, and steered for the river bank.

"What is it Cuddles, what have you heard?" Nelly asked again.

"Dogs!" came the reply.

"Dogs?" queried Nelly, not understanding the significance of her friend's statement.

"Yes, dogs, and sheep, over there," he nodded in the direction from which he had heard the sounds. "There's a flock in trouble. We must help them." As soon as the raft had reached the river bank, the three animals leapt off. "Secure the raft, Gloucester, and then follow us," ordered Cuddles. "Come on Nelly, we're the fastest, we'll go on ahead. There isn't a moment to lose."

They raced off, leaving Gloucester to moor the raft. As they ran, Nelly began to hear the sounds of dogs barking, and more, much more. The sound of sheep bleating could be clearly heard, screaming in panic and fear, and the cries of terrified lambs. Eventually, the source of all the commotion could clearly be seen, and a terrible sight it was too. The flock was running en masse, being chased by three dogs. At a distance it looked like a large white flag being waved against a green background as the frightened sheep ran back and forth across the field.

As the two companions drew nearer, they could see the dogs running by the side of the flock, biting and worrying the sheep on the outside, pulling at their wool and legs. One dog even managed to bring one of the ewes down but, fortunately, she was able to free herself from the dog's jaws and return to the comparative safety of the flock before the other dogs could pounce on her. The two companions were filled with a mixture of emotions; the sickening spectacle revolted them and, at the same time, a feeling of hopelessness and desperation as they watched, still too far away to help stop the carnage, on they ran.

As they entered the field where the sheep were, they could see that the dogs had trapped the flock in a corner and were beginning to close in for the kill. Then, from within the massed ranks of the flock, a solitary sheep stepped forward. It was a large ram. He walked slowly towards the dogs, stamping his feet on the ground in defiance as he went. The three dogs began to circle him, the hair on their backs raised, growling as they bared their teeth.

"He hasn't got a chance," cried Cuddles, desperately. As they drew nearer to the gallant ram, the dogs attacked and, although he fought bravely, he was overwhelmed by the sheer number of the brutes. One dog seized his leg, while another bit him hard on the back of the neck, and the third pulled hard on the wool at his flanks, dragging him to the floor. Nelly glanced over to Cuddles, who was showing no sign of fear as he raced to his kinsman's aid. Nelly, who had never been confronted with such violence in her life, although frightened, was determined to do what she could to help, and pressed on.

"You take the one on the right, and I'll take the one on the left," instructed Cuddles.

When they reached the stricken ram, they hurled themselves at their respective targets, butting them as hard as they could with their heads, sending the two dogs

43

sprawling to the ground. The third dog, seeing what had happened to his partners in crime, released his grip on the ram, allowing him to get up.

The dog that Nelly had butted was quickly to his feet and stared hard at his attacker. He was a large black dog, powerfully built, but the most distinguishing feature about him was a scar that ran almost down the middle of his face, from his ear, between his eyes, and almost to his nose; it gave him a most menacing appearance. Nelly tried to return his stare, but found her adversary too formidable. The dog was quick to realise that Nelly was afraid of him, and made the most of his advantage. He curled his lips up to display his vicious teeth.

"Goat tastes just as good as sheep," he growled, his voice full of cruelty and venom as he walked menacingly towards Nelly.

"Be off with you," replied Nelly, trying her best to sound brave, but in truth, she was terrified. The dog laughed an evil laugh at her.

"Say goodbye little goat," he snarled, and leapt at her. Frozen with fear, Nelly closed her eyes and instinctively lowered her head. A terrible scream of pain could be heard as the dog threw himself onto Nelly's sharp horns. The great weight of the dog on her head made Nelly buckle at the knees, and she sank to the floor. For a moment the dog writhed in agony, impaled on the horns; then, despite the obvious pain, and with great strength, he pushed himself away from Nelly, pulling the horns out of his shoulder. He stood there panting, with blood streaming from his wounds, and stared hard at Nelly.

"I'm going to remember you, little goat," he hissed. "Be sure, we'll meet again, and next time you won't be so lucky." And with that he turned and limped away, leaving a trail of blood behind him.

Nelly suddenly felt very faint. Her head was spinning and she was trembling all over, obviously in a state of shock.

For a while she seemed to lose all sense of what was happening around her. It was as if she were in a dream: she thought she heard a voice, a very distant voice, calling her name.

"Nelly, are you all right?" it asked. "Nelly, come on, snap out of it, it's all over, the dogs have gone." She slowly came out of her daze, to see that it had been Cuddles who had been talking to her.

"Are you all right?" he asked again, very concerned.

"I think so," replied Nelly uncertainly.

"You look dreadful," commented Cuddles, who could see that his friend was far from being all right. "Come and sit down here, in the shade, and rest a while." He led his dazed companion to an old tree and sat her down beneath it. She gazed vacantly out into space, still not sure of where she was, or what had happened. Cuddles, still very concerned, spoke to her again.

"You've got blood on your horns, old girl. I think you should wipe it off," he said gently. This seemed to shake Nelly out of her trance, making her cringe with disgust at the thought of having that awful dog's blood on her, and she promptly wiped her horns clean on the grass.

"What happened?" she asked, after regaining her composure.

"Can't you remember?" Cuddles enquired.

"Not all of it," admitted Nelly.

"Well," began Cuddles "after we had knocked those two dogs off, the third took fright and ran, leaving me and Boris here to beat up the other one. Oh, by the way, this is Boris." Cuddles introduced the ram they had saved, to Nelly, and "hellos" were exchanged, before Cuddles continued. "As we were taking care of him, so to speak, we heard this terrible scream, and looked round to see that big black dog stuck on your horns. Unfortunately, as we were watching you, our fellow escaped or we'd have given him a thrashing that he would never forget."

"I don't think your dog will ever forget what happened to him today," Boris remarked to Nelly.

"No, he said he wouldn't," replied Nelly, who felt a shiver run down her spine as she remembered the dog's threat.

"Oh, that's just talk. We'll never see him again," predicted Cuddles confidently. "And while we're on the subject of not seeing certain animals, have you noticed that a certain pig is nowhere to be seen?"

"Gloucester, of course. Where can he be?" pondered Nelly.

"Lost, probably. He should have been here ages ago," Cuddles was quick to point out. They all gazed in the general direction from which Gloucester should have come, but there was still no sign of him.

By now the flock had gathered around their heroes, thanking them and singing their praises. Cuddles quite enjoyed all the attention, while Nelly was her usual modest self about it all. Fortunately, none of the sheep had received any serious injuries, only a few cuts and bruises, although Boris did have a nasty cut above one eye and had received a bite on the leg, but nothing that wouldn't heal with time.

After fifteen minutes or so of reliving the morning's events and attending to Boris's injuries, a small lamb was spotted racing across the field. He dashed to his mother and, with great urgency, told her something that was obviously of the utmost importance. The ewe in turn passed the message on to Boris, who nodded his head in interest as she spoke. When she had finished, he turned to Nelly and Cuddles.

"This friend of yours wouldn't happen to be a large spotted pig, would he?"

"The very one," exclaimed Cuddles.

"Why, what has he done?" always expecting the worst of Gloucester.

"It appears he's just in the next field, sitting down," Boris informed them.

"Typical," tutted Cuddles. "Here we are, risking life and limb, while he spends the day lazing around."

"Not exactly" interrupted Boris. "You see, he's sitting on a dog ... the same dog that ran off."

"What!" exclaimed Cuddles in amazement.

"Good old Gloucester!" cried Nelly.

"Excuse me, Sir," butted in the lamb who had originally brought the message, "but Mister Gloucester told me to tell these kind animals to ... and these are his exact words, not mine ... to 'get off their backsides and lend a hand'. That's what he said, honest." The lamb looked very coy, but then, remembering something else, added "He also said something about being stuck there all day, but I didn't quite catch it all."

"That sounds like Gloucester," confirmed Nelly. Boris told the lamb that he had done very well, and patted him on the head. The lamb then returned to his proud mother, feeling very pleased with himself.

"I suppose," said Cuddles, rising to his feet, "we had better go and see what our spotted friend has captured."

They crossed the field, and into the next where they saw Gloucester who, as they had been told, was sitting on a very unhappy dog.

"And about time too," said Gloucester upon seeing his companions. "I've been here for ages. I thought no-one was ever going to come."

"Er, what you got there Gloucester?" joked Cuddles.

"Well, what does it look like!" retorted Gloucester, in a bit of a huff.

"W-e-l-l, it looks a bit like a dog," answered Nelly, joining in the fun. "But it's a bit hard to tell, being covered by so much pig."

"Of course it's a ..." Gloucester, seeing that the others were pulling his leg, began to smile broadly.

"Please let me go," begged the dog, pitifully.

"Shut up!" ordered Gloucester, who bounced hard upon

his prisoner, making him groan in discomfort.

"He doesn't look very comfortable, does he?" gibed Cuddles.

"Please, I'm very sorry," wailed the dog. "I didn't mean any harm. I didn't even want to chase the sheep. Scar made me do it."

"What did you say?" demanded Cuddles, with all the humour now gone from his voice.

"Scar made me. He said if we didn't help him, he'd turn on us. I'm so sorry," cried the dog.

"Scar," muttered Cuddles, lost in thought. "After all these years, and to think that I was so close to him."

"You know him then, this Scar?" asked Nelly, seeing that the news had troubled her friend.

"Oh yes, I know him," replied Cuddles slowly. "It was him who killed my mother."

The company was struck dumb by this tragic news, nobody quite able to find any suitable words for such an occasion. It was Cuddles himself who broke the uneasy silence, telling Gloucester to get up off the unhappy dog. The dog rose stiffly to his feet, and Cuddles began to question him.

"Where is he now? Scar, I mean?"

"I don't know," replied the dog, looking nervously about him, still unsure as to what his fate might be. Cuddles was not pleased with this answer, and frowned hard.

"Look dog, you're in a lot of trouble, and if you don't answer our questions, things are only going to get worse for you," threatened Gloucester, trying to frighten the already terrified dog even further.

"Honest, I don't know," repeated the dog desperately.

"But he's a friend of yours, isn't he, so you must know where he lives?" reasoned Gloucester.

"I hardly know him. I only met him a couple of days ago," explained the dog.

Cuddles suggested that the dog start at the beginning

and give an exact account of the events that had brought him to his present predicament. The dog took a deep breath and began his story,

"It was two days ago. My friend Bobby and I were playing in the wood, you know, just messing about doing no harm to anybody, when all of a sudden this dog jumped out of the undergrowth. It was Scar. He seemed very cross with us, and said that if we didn't do as we were told he'd bite us ... well, what he actually said was that he'd tear us apart. We were both very frightened of him. He looked so big and savage, what with that scar and all; we were afraid to disobey him. We just stayed there in the wood, and when it came time to go home, he wouldn't let us go. The next morning, we asked him again if we could go home, saying we were hungry and that our owners would be missing us. But all he said was for us not to be such a pair of babies, and that there would be plenty to eat tomorrow. All day, he kept asking us if there were any chicken houses locally, or flocks of sheep. We told him about this flock, but we had no idea what he had in mind. By this morning, we were very hungry. I remember he smiled that cruel smile and said "All right boys, we'll go and eat." He made us show him where the flock was, and told us how to chase them. Neither Bobby nor myself wanted to, and said so. He became very angry, saying that he'd eaten cowardly dogs before now, and that if we didn't help him catch a sheep, he would eat us, and I think he meant it. We were so afraid of him that we did as he asked, but we didn't want to, honestly. Then you two turned up, and you know the rest."

The assembled company considered the dog's story, and after a certain amount of discussion decided to let the dog go free, all of them being of the opinion that he had been as much a victim of Scar as they had.

"But promise us that you will never do anything like it again," demanded Cuddles sternly. The dog duly promised, and was allowed to go on his way.

50

That night the flock threw a big party in honour of their heroes. Little lambs were brought to meet the honoured guests by their mothers. It was wonderful. Gloucester revelled in all the attention, relating his story of how he single-handedly caught a savage dog, to anyone who would listen.

"It was like this." he began, addressing a captive audience. "After I had tied up the raft, I ran after Nelly and Cuddles, but as you can see I'm not quite as agile as those two." He rubbed his large tummy, and winked at one of the lambs, who giggled ... only to be cuffed about the head by his mother for being disrespectful. "So I got left behind a bit. It's a long way from the river to your field, and to be honest I ran out of puff, so I stopped for a moment beside that tree, just to catch my breath. Well, blow me, if I didn't look up and see this dog coming my way. I assumed it must be one of the dogs that we were after. I hid behind the tree, so he wouldn't see me, and, as he ran past, I jumped out and pinned him to the ground before he knew what had happened. There we stayed until this clever little chap found us." The lamb who had brought the message back was now sitting beside Gloucester, feeling very proud of himself.

Nelly, modest as ever, tried to play down her part in the incident, although, without a doubt, it was she who had been in the greatest danger of all of them. She received their praise and gratitude with her customary 'thank you' and 'you're too kind.'

As the revelry continued, Nelly noticed that Cuddles had disappeared from the party, and went to look for him. She found him standing beneath a tree, staring into the night, deep in thought. Walking slowly up to him, she stood in silence by his side. Although neither said anything for a few minutes, Nelly knew what her friend was thinking.

"Are you all right?" she asked him quietly.

"I just wanted to be alone for a while," he replied, still deep in thought.

"It might help if you talked about it," suggested Nelly delicately.

"About what?" queried Cuddles.

"Your mother," replied Nelly. "It was her you were thinking about, wasn't it?" Cuddles turned his head and half-smiled and said, "You're a wise animal, Nelly. It's been a while since I thought about her, but what happened today brought it all flooding back.

"It seems so long ago," continued Cuddles thoughtfully, "but I remember it all, as if it were only yesterday. It was a lovely spring day and I was only a lamb, running and playing, as lambs do, without a care in the world. Mother told me to follow her down to the stream, as she was thirsty. While she drank, I looked in the water and saw another lamb looking at me, but mother said it was only my reflection, and there wasn't another in the whole world like me, and that she loved me dearly. It was she who named me Cuddles. Stupid name, really, but I've always kept it in memory of her, though heaven knows the amount of mickey-taking I've suffered because of it!. Suddenly we heard the sound of dogs barking. I didn't understand what it all meant, but mother knew straight away. She told me to stay close to her, and we ran back to the flock. It was terrible: dogs chasing the sheep, cruel, vicious dogs." He paused and shuddered, still unable to recount the full horror of what had happened that fateful day, all those years ago.

"I tried to stay by mother's side, but in all the confusion we were separated. On and on the dogs kept chasing, until I was exhausted, my legs felt like lead, and my lungs were fit to burst. Despite all my efforts to stay with the main flock, I began to lag behind. It was then I saw him. Even to this day I can clearly see that evil black face, with a scar running down it."

"The same dog we saw today," commented Nelly.

"Yes, the very same dog, still up to his murderous tricks after all these years," confirmed Cuddles, before continuing. "As I said, the dog spotted me falling behind the rest, and moved in for the kill. He was nearly on top of me, ready to pounce, when the sound of gunfire was heard. Obviously he knew all about guns, because as soon as he heard the shots he stopped chasing me and ran off. It was the farmer who was shooting: in fact he shot all the other dogs, but Scar got away. Later I learned that mother was one of those who had been killed in the raid, leaving me an orphan. The farmer took me home with him, and as I was too young to look after myself, his daughter fed me on the bottle. The strange thing was that my best friend when I was a pet lamb was Tess, the sheepdog. She felt sorry for me and at first I was afraid of her, but soon came to realise that she meant me no harm, and quickly came to trust her. At night she would jump into my pen and I would snuggle up to her, as I had with my mother. It was Tess who told me that all dogs aren't bad, in fact very few are."

"So that's why you let that dog go this morning?" interrupted Nelly, who had found her friend's benevolence earlier that day a bit strange.

"He wasn't a bad dog," explained Cuddles, "only foolish, being led on by that devil Scar. He won't do it again, I'm sure of that. But Scar's a different matter. He'll do it again and again, forcing others weaker than himself to help in his mayhem ... that dog is evil, truly evil. He must be stopped and if needs be, destroyed or he will continue to spread his poison wherever he goes.

"You know, I was talking to a cockerel last year who told me that a chicken house had been raided near him some weeks before, by a dog answering Scar's description. A lot of hens were killed, but the farmer disturbed the dog and actually shot him; then he got up and ran off. It's almost as if the Devil himself protects him, but I swear that one day I will meet up with that black-hearted fiend, and kill him. Not just for my mother, but for all the other lambs he's made orphans, for all the ewes that have wept over lost lambs after one of his raids, for all the chickens he has killed, and the geese that have mourned their goslings; for all of them, I swear I will destroy that monster ... if it's the last thing I ever do!" Nelly looked into her friend's eyes, and saw something that frightened her: pure hate!

At the same time as the two friends were talking, a large dog limped into a wood some miles away. His shoulder and leg matted in dried blood, he slumped to the floor and began to lick his wounds. The rabbits ran instinctively for the safety of their burrows, owls took to the wing, bats swerved to avoid the area, as if they sensed the presence of some terrible evil that had visited them. The dog gazed out into the darkness; the scar that ran down his face seemed to burn red with rage.

"One day" he snarled to himself "one day, little goat,

I'll tear your throat out. No matter how long it takes, or how far I have to travel, I swear I'll get even with you."

* * * * *

The next morning the entire flock came down to the river to see the animals off. Boris once again extended an invitation to Cuddles to stay with them but, as he had the previous evening, declined the offer.

"It's very kind of you," said Cuddles "and very tempting, but I must stay with my friends, at least until we find the sea. It's so very important to Nelly."

"Perhaps when your quest is over, you may consider returning to us. You know you'll always be welcome," suggested Boris.

"We'll see," came the reply.

As the raft floated down the river, the three animals waved goodbye to their new friends. A few lambs skipped along the river bank, keeping pace with the raft until concerned mothers ordered them back.

"Do you think they'll be all right now?" Nelly asked Cuddles, as they watched the flock disappear into the distance.

"They should be. The shepherd knows what happened, so he'll be on his guard from now on."

"Wish you'd stayed?" she asked him.

"Yes and no. They're a smashing bunch of sheep, and I did like Boris, but I looked at it this way: if I had stayed, who on earth was going to look after you two?" Cuddles winked at Nelly. "The idea of you and Gloucester let loose on the countryside without supervision doesn't bear thinking about."

CHAPTER FOUR : PIGNAPPED

It had always been the practice of the three animals to eat a hearty breakfast each morning before setting off on the next leg of their journey, as was the case one particular sunny dawn. They strolled casually along the river bank, each looking for something tasty to eat. Nelly soon found an elder bush, heavy with leaves, much to her liking, and Cuddles a patch of clover. Gloucester on the other hand felt like a change from his usual diet of roots, and continued his foray alone. After ten minutes of finding nothing that really took his fancy, he came upon a road. Normally he would have avoided this thoroughfare, but he noticed a brown paper sack on the side of the road; he looked and pondered.

"I wonder what's in it?" he thought to himself.

He considered turning back, knowing that men used such byways. It had always been the policy to avoid humans as much as possible, but his curiosity grew as he looked at the sack.

"It wouldn't do any harm, to just nip over a take a peek," he said to himself, and quickly dashed over to the sack. As he reached it, he noticed that it was torn, revealing its contents: potatoes. Now potatoes featured high in Gloucester's list of favourite foods, second only to acorns, and he couldn't remember the last time he had tasted one. He squealed with joy as he ripped the bag open and began to devour its contents, with all thought of where he was now gone completely out of his head. He had eaten nearly half of the contents when, suddenly, he was grabbed from behind by two men. He had been so engrossed with his breakfast that he had failed to hear them creep up on him. He fought as best he could, but the men were very strong and dragged him to a van that was parked nearby where, after a lot of squealing on the part of Gloucester and cursing on the part of the men, he was thrown unceremoniously into the back of the van, and the doors locked.

After their exertions the two men leaned against the van to catch their breath.

"That's a bit of luck, eh, Bert," commented one of the men.

"Just a bit," replied Bert. "And he should bring a few pounds at auction."

"Auction!" thought Gloucester, swallowing hard as the van drove off into the distance, with a large protesting pig in the back.

\* \* \* \* \* \*

"Most inconsiderate of him," said Cuddles irritably. Both he and Nelly had been waiting for nearly an hour at the raft for Gloucester to return.

"I wonder where he can be?" asked Nelly, who was becoming a little concerned as to the whereabouts of the third member of their party.

"Probably lost or stuck down a hole, knowing him," replied Cuddles.

They waited another hour or so, then decided to go and look for him. A good part of the morning was taken up with the search, which revealed nothing, until they came upon the road and the half-eaten bag of potatoes.

"Well, he's been here," observed Cuddles, examining the bag, "that's for sure."

Nelly agreed. "But where is he now?"

"Strange he should have left these potatoes, without finishing them first," added Cuddles. They both stood there pondering the mystery, when a little voice was heard up above.

"Can I help you?" it squeaked.

Nelly and Cuddles looked up to see a squirrel addressing them from the branches of a tree.

"Are you looking for something?" he enquired, staring down at them.

"We're looking for our friend. You haven't seen him, have you?" Nelly asked him.

"Maybe. What does he look like?"

"He's a pig," Cuddles butted in.

"Large pig, covered in black spots?" asked the squirrel.

"That's the one," confirmed Cuddles. "You've seen him then."

"Oh yes, earlier this morning. He was eating those potatoes which had fallen off a lorry last night."

"We can all see he's been here, but where is he now?" demanded Cuddles, getting a bit annoyed.

"Two men came and picked him up, and took him off in their van," the squirrel informed them in a matter-of-fact manner.

"WHAT!" exclaimed the two animals at once. "WHEN?"

The squirrel thought hard before answering, "Three or four hours ago, maybe more."

The two animals continued to question the squirrel further but were unable to gain any more useful information as to where their friend might be at that particular moment. They wandered back to the raft, very depressed, considering what to do next.

"We've got to look for him," said Nelly adamantly.

"I agree," confirmed Cuddles, "but where do we start looking? He could be anywhere." They sat down and discussed all possibilities.

"We know he was taken in a van," Nelly pointed out, "which means he's gone by road."

"True," replied Cuddles, "but that doesn't help us much. There are miles and miles of roads. He could be a hundred miles away by now."

The more they thought about it, the more the prospect of finding Gloucester seemed less likely, but they both agreed at least to try.

Over the next week they walked many miles in their search, and questioned all the animals they met in the hope that one of them had seen their friend, but all to no avail. There was one occasion when their hopes were raised, when a cow told them that she had seen a pig wandering around locally but, sadly for Nelly and Cuddles, it turned out to be a local pig just out for a stroll.

At the end of the week it was becoming obvious, even to Nelly, that they were not going to find their lost companion.

"We have to face it, he's gone," said Cuddles, as sympathetically as possible to Nelly.

"I know," replied a disconsolate Nelly. "Poor Gloucester. Where can he be?"

Cuddles persuaded Nelly that it would be best to continue their journey without Gloucester, pointing out that it wasn't doing anyone any good staying in the area. Nelly of course wanted to stay a little longer in the hope that Gloucester may, even at this late hour, somehow return to them, but in the end she had to agree with Cuddles. Nelly sat on the raft and cried uncontrollably, as Cuddles launched the raft, and steered them to the middle of the river. Neither said anything, neither could, and even with Cuddles's strength of character, he found it hard to fight back the tears.

\* \* \* \* \*

Gloucester had no way of knowing how many miles he had travelled in the back of the van, but it seemed to him to be a very long time. Nor had he any idea where he was going. Finally, after what seemed like hours, the van stopped and the door opened. Gloucester found himself in a farmyard, and a rather untidy one at that. The yard itself was dirty, looking as if it hadn't been swept for years, and farm buildings derelict. The two men dragged Gloucester roughly from the back of the van, marched him across the yard, and threw him into an old dilapidated pigsty.

Bewildered and dazed he just sat there, convinced that it was all a bad dream and that he would wake up at any moment. But, of course, it wasn't. The pigsty itself was a shabby affair. It had a hard concrete floor, that felt cold against his skin when he tried to lie down. What little straw there was, was dirty and hardly enough for him to make the crudest of beds. The roof was in a state of disrepair and had a large hole in it that had let rain in over many years, resulting in a large patch of green mould growing on the wall directly beneath it. Gloucester considered this to be the worst place he had ever seen in his life, let alone been asked to stay in.

He neither saw nor heard anyone or anything for the remainder of the day but, as it started to grow dark, one of his captors came to see him bringing a bucket which Gloucester hoped contained his supper. Having not eaten since that morning he was now very hungry. The man emptied the contents of the bucket into an old cracked trough. To Gloucester's dismay, it was made up of old potatoes, carrots, parsnips, apples and other types of fruit and vegetables, most of which were rotten, and even Gloucester, as hungry as he was, could not bring himself to eat the disgusting mess and turned his nose up at it.

"Ungrateful pig!" cursed the man, who then kicked Gloucester on the shoulder, making him retreat to the back of the sty to avoid any more kicks.

The night passed very slowly for Gloucester. He was unable to sleep on the cold hard floor, and a draught blew in on him through a small hole in the wall. Never before had he felt so depressed or alone, imprisoned in his squalid sty, miles from anywhere, uncertain of what tomorrow might bring. From where he was sitting the future looked very bleak indeed. He thought of his friends, who he was sure would be out at that very moment looking for him, with little chance of finding him so far from the river. He began to realise that he would probably never see them again, making him even more depressed. He looked up through the hole in the pigsty roof, gazed at the stars that twinkled in the night sky, and began to pray.

"Dear God," he began, in a low solemn voice. "Take pity on a poor stupid pig, and return me to the safety of my friends, Nelly and Cuddles. I promise that in future I will be a good pig, and never again be greedy or selfish." The tears ran freely down his chubby face; a sad and lonely pig.

The next morning, soon after dawn, the two men reversed the van to the door of the old pigsty and once again bundled Gloucester into the back of it, and drove off. This journey however, was much shorter than the one the previous day, and it wasn't long before they reached their destination.

When the van doors opened for Gloucester to be unloaded, he found he was at what he later learned to be an auction. It seemed to Gloucester to be a cold, unfriendly place, all concrete and steel, full of noises that echoed in the vast expanses of the high tin roof that covered the entire area. Amid this crescendo of noise, Gloucester could make out a few familiar sounds: in the distance cows could be heard mooing, also the bleats of lambs, and the squeals of pigs, men shouting and swearing, the crash of steel gates as they slammed against steel posts, and many other sounds, indistinguishable amidst the bedlam. On the other side of the auction Gloucester could see cattle being unloaded from cattle wagons, herded down alleyways by men with sticks and driven into steel pens. The whole scene seemed one of total chaos. Gloucester took an instant dislike to the place.

The two men who had brought Gloucester pulled him out of the van, chased him down an alleyway and onto what turned out to be a weighing machine. He stayed there for a couple of minutes while he was weighed, and his weight duly noted. From there he was driven down another alleyway into a waiting pen, alongside a lot of other pigs. It was fortunate in as much as the pen in which Gloucester found himself was indoors, as was the case with all the pig pens, and had been bedded down with fresh clean straw, which Gloucester began to eat. Although somewhat tasteless, it went some way to ease the hunger pains that Gloucester was now feeling, having not eaten for a full twenty-four hours. As he ate, he looked at the other occupants in the adjoining pens, all of which looked either frightened or depressed. In a pen further down the line, he could hear a pig sobbing.

"What are we doing here?" he heard another cry in the distance. A Landrace told him to be quiet, whilst another tried to comfort him with kind words, all to no avail. Gloucester introduced himself to his immediate neighbour, a Large White called Fred.

"Where are we?" Gloucester asked him.

"At the auction," replied Fred, somewhat surprised at the question.

Gloucester's heart sank; he had heard of auctions, and what happened there. "So we're to be sold then," said Gloucester, gloomily stating the obvious.

"Very likely," confirmed his neighbour, who almost found Gloucester's remarks amusing but, under the circumstances, not quite. Gloucester remained silent, unable to think of anything to say, as was the case with all the pigs, none of which were feeling very sociable. Occasionally men would climb into the pens to look at the pigs. Quite a few looked at Gloucester, their faces hard, and their stares cold and calculating.

After an hour or so, a large crowd congregated around the pig pens. Gloucester knew that something was about to happen. He heard a man ring a bell, and shout, "Pig buyers, pig buyers, come on you pig buyers, let's make a start!" A man in a white coat, carrying a heavy stick, walked down the alleyway talking to the other men as he did so, climbed up onto a walkway directly above the pens and made his way to Gloucester's pen. "Right, gentlemen," he said, addressing the crowd that had collected in front of Gloucester, "Shall we make a start? Lot One, a Gloucester Old Spot, and what a fine looking specimen he is too." The man prodded Gloucester with his stick, making him move around his pen, so that potential customers could get a good look at him, before continuing "Yes indeed, and a good weight too: plenty of sausages and bacon on this fellow, for sure."

"Sausages! Bacon!" thought Gloucester, alarmed, as the seriousness of his predicament suddenly became clear to him.

The auctioneer continued, "Now what am I bid for this fine pig. Who'll start me at fifty pounds? Fifty pounds, someone surely, thank you, sir. Fifty pounds I am bid, who'll say fifty-five?" A man in a blue and white striped coat raised his finger.

"Fifty-five pounds bid." The auctioneer kept taking the bids from the crowd; "Sixty pounds now, sixty-five, seventy pounds, seventy-two on my right, seventy-four, seventy-six. Your bid now, Sir, Yes! No! Yes, thank you. Seventy-eight bid, have you all finished, I'm selling now at seventy-eight pounds ... sold to Mr Jones the butcher, for seventy-eight pounds!" and banged his stick against the bars to close the bidding.

"Butcher!" gulped Gloucester, who suddenly felt very faint.

The auctioneer continued down the line, selling the pigs as he went, though Gloucester was far too stunned to take any interest in the proceedings. All that kept ringing in his ear was "Seventy-eight pounds, Jones, the butcher."

When the sale was over, an uncomfortable silence descended upon the pig pens. Again none of the occupants had anything to say. Now and then some man or other came and took a pig out of its pen and drove it away. Gloucester waited for his purchaser to come, but for a long time he had to remain in his pen. He was beginning to hope that the butcher had forgotten all about him, and had visions of being set free, on account that nobody wanted him: a vain hope, but in that situation vain hopes were better than none at all.

Sadly Gloucester's new owner finally arrived to take him away. He was walked out of the pig section, and loaded into the back of a van. This van was an improvement on the one that Gloucester had arrived in, but it was still a van, and still a means by which to deny him his freedom.

It appeared at first glance that Gloucester had been the butcher's only purchase that day, because the van was empty except for Gloucester. There was however a sack in one corner, which obviously had something in it. Gloucester went over and investigated, in the hope that there might be something to eat. He nuzzled the bag, which suddenly moved, causing Gloucester to jump. He touched it again, and once more it moved. "I wonder what it can be," thought Gloucester to himself. The bag was tied at the top with string, which Gloucester decided to untie, curiosity getting the better of him; he tugged at the string with his teeth, which quickly came undone. Suddenly a white head, which had a yellow beak attached to it, popped out of the bag and pecked Gloucester hard on the nose.

"Ouch!" cried Gloucester, retreating to the back of the van, with his nose throbbing.

"Take that!" hissed his attacker.

"What did you do that for!" demanded Gloucester, rubbing his nose.

"Come any nearer, and you'll get another one," threatened the other, who hopped out of the bag.

Gloucester could now see that his attacker was a large white goose, who was obviously in a bad mood, on account that he kept hissing at Gloucester. Unsure as to how to handle his aggressive discovery, Gloucester tried to reason with him, in the hope that he wouldn't receive any more painful pecks.

"I don't know why you're taking it out on me," he began, "after all it was me who let you out of the sack in the first place." The goose considered what Gloucester had said.

"True" he replied, "but I wasn't to know that you weren't the man, was I? It was him who stuck me in the bag in the first place."

"Well I'm not, and I didn't," Gloucester pointed out, "and anyway we shouldn't be fighting. It seems we're both in the same predicament. We should be working together to get ourselves out of here."

"Good point." agreed the goose without hesitation, then thought for a moment before adding in a somewhat uncertain tone, "What exactly is our predicament?"

"We're in this van," replied Gloucester, somewhat puzzled at the question.

"I know that," snapped the goose "but what will happen when we get out of here?"

"For goodness sake!" wailed Gloucester. "We've been bought by a butcher."

"Oh!" replied the goose, looking somewhat puzzled. "What's a butcher?"

Gloucester closed his eyes and shook his head in despair.

"You don't know what a butcher is?" The goose shook his head.

"Let me see, how can I put it?" groaned Gloucester, wearily. "If we don't escape, by this time tomorrow I'll be a pile of sausages and bacon and you'll be somebody's Sunday dinner."

"What!" screeched the goose, flying up into the air, banging his head on the roof.

"Afraid so," added Gloucester. "So you can see what I mean about working together to get out of here."

"Too right," agreed the goose, shaking his sore head. "What are we going to do?"

"I wish I knew," said Gloucester despondently.

"I know!" screeched the goose triumphantly. "When he

opens the door, I'll attack him, I'll soon sort him out. Sunday dinner indeed!"

The goose then proceeded to strut about, describing in some detail what he was going to do to the butcher. All of which Gloucester found very tedious, when suddenly he had an idea.

"A sharp peck on the ear," continued the goose, "or a bash on the head with my wing, should do the trick, followed by ..."

"Will you shut up and listen?" bellowed Gloucester, who had tried unsuccessfully to attract the goose's attention for at least a minute. The goose ceased his theatricals, and gave Gloucester his undivided attention. "As far as I can see," began Gloucester, "we've only one chance of escape. You must get back into the sack."

"What!" protested the goose. "Back in there! Why?"

"Because that's where the butcher will expect you to be," explained Gloucester. "He'll never suspect for a moment that I would have untied the string, so when he opens the doors he'll expect you to be where he'd left you, in the bag. Of course I won't tie it up, but he shouldn't notice that. Now, and this is the important bit, when he does open the doors, I'll shout 'GO': you then fly out of the bag and attack the butcher. He'll be so surprised at first that he'll be unable to do anything, and by the time he's recovered his senses, I'll be sitting on him!"

"Then what?" asked the goose."Then we run for it," replied Gloucester deliberately, trying to keep his composure.

"Sounds good to me," agreed the goose, "especially the bit about me attacking the butcher. I really like the sound of that."

As they travelled from the auction to the butcher's home, the plan was gone over again and again, to be sure each knew exactly what the other had to do. The more they discussed it, the more the goose liked it, the violent parts in particular.

The van finally drew to a halt and positions were taken up, with the goose in his sack and Gloucester as far away from the doors as possible. As the door opened Gloucester cowered away, trying to look as frightened as he could, which wasn't difficult.

The butcher leaned forward in an attempt to grab the reluctant pig, then when he was almost touching him, Gloucester cried "GO!". The goose heard his cue, and flew out of his sack and into the butcher's face, pecking him about the head and flapping his wings violently, boxing the man's ears as he did so. Gloucester seized his opportunity, leapt out of the van and onto the butcher, sending all three sprawling to the ground.

Once certain that he had the butcher well and truly pinned to the floor, Gloucester proceeded to bounce up and down on him. It was at that precise moment that Gloucester finally lost his temper. It was as if the events of the past two days had combined in finally bringing an eruption of fury from him.

"I've just about had enough!" he roared, staring into the butcher's reddening face, only inches from his. "There's only so much a pig can take, and I've taken all I'm going to take! First I'm stolen, taken forcibly from my friends, driven halfway across the country, forced to sleep in a squalid little pigsty, offered nothing to eat except a bucket of rotten fruit and vegetables, hawked off to an auction, weighed, prodded and poked by every Tom, Dick and Harry, sold, stuck in a van, pecked on the nose by a half-crazed goose, but do you know what really annoys me?" By now he was bellowing at the butcher, who had turned a bright scarlet. "What really annoys me is the fact that I only made seventy-eight pounds! That is an insult! I'll have you know that I'm a Pedigree Gloucester Old Spot, with a family tree that can be traced back over a hundred years, which I'm sure is something you can't do, and to suggest that I'm only worth a miserable seventy-eight quid is … is … is an affront to my family name!"

He was finally brought to his senses by a sharp peck on the ear by the goose.

"Are you coming?" he screeched at Gloucester "or do you intend to stay there all day?" Gloucester, realising that his vocal outburst was jeopardizing their escape, quickly regained his wits.

"It's all right," he assured the goose, "I've cooled down now."

"Then let's get going!" urged the goose. Gloucester gave the butcher one more bounce, for good measure, and ran for the road, closely followed by the goose. They ran down the road for a mile or so, without meeting any traffic, before Gloucester realised something.

"Quick!" he yelled, "We must get off this public highway. Men are always on it. One might come along at any moment." Even as he spoke they could hear the noise of a vehicle behind them. "That's probably the butcher looking for us now." They both looked for a way to leave the road.

"Over there!" screeched the goose, who ran over to a wooden gate that had been left ajar. Gloucester quickly followed. They had only just managed to hide behind the hedge, when the butcher's van drove past.

"That was a near thing," sighed Gloucester, before turning to his associate. "The further we get away from here the better," to which the goose agreed.

They either ran or jogged for the rest of the day, not with any particular destination in mind, just trying to put as many miles between themselves and the butcher as possible. Eventually as night fell, they stopped in a small wood, tired and hungry.

## CHAPTER FIVE : PIGS MAY FLY

The next morning, both Gloucester and the goose slept late, after the exertions of the previous day, not waking up until nearly noon but when they did, both were ravenous, having not eaten for some considerable time. Gloucester rummaged around, until he found some tasty roots, while the goose pulled at the lush grass. When both were full and satisfied, they considered what was best to do next.

"I must find the river, and my friends," said Gloucester adamantly.

"What friends on the river?" asked the goose, unaware of such matters. Although they had been allies for nearly twenty-four hours, neither knew anything about the other, and the goose had no idea as to the events that had brought Gloucester to his present predicament, so they sat down, and Gloucester told him his story.

"You've had quite a time of it," said the goose, who'd decided not to relate an account of how he had reached the auction, as it seemed rather boring compared to Gloucester's tales. In fact his journey was the first he'd ever made, having never left the farm where he had hatched.

"I have, so you see I really must get back to my friends, who are probably worried sick by now," confirmed Gloucester, who had returned to his old self and was full of his own importance.

"But where is the river?" asked the goose. "If what you say is true about travelling in that van for hours, we could be miles away, and what's more, we don't even know in what direction to go."

What the goose had said was perfectly true, and Gloucester knew it. They could set off in totally the wrong direction, taking them even further away. To Gloucester the problem seemed insurmountable.

"Well, one thing's for sure," said Gloucester, finally deciding to make a decision, "we can't stay here. That butcher might still be looking for us. I suggest we carry on in the same direction as we did last night, and ask anyone we meet if they know the way to the river, if that's all right with you?"

"Suits me just fine," replied the goose, who was rather hoping Gloucester would ask him to tag along. The pig's tales of adventure had whetted his appetite, and he was sure that it would only be a question of time before some new escapade developed.

For a whole week, Gloucester and the goose travelled in search of the river, questioning all the animals they met: rabbits, squirrels, cows and on one occasion, the wisest of all woodland creatures, the badger. It was quite obvious that they were a very long way from the river, and even Gloucester was beginning to doubt whether he would ever see his friends again, until the first and only ray of hope occurred, late one afternoon. They were passing a pond, where three wild Mallard ducks were feeding.

"Excuse me!" shouted Gloucester, addressing the ducks. "I wonder if you could help me? I'm looking for a river. Would you know if there's one near here?"

"Maybe we do, maybe we don't," replied one of the ducks, sarcastically, who then turned to his friends and giggled.

"Strange bird," Gloucester remarked to the goose.

"Hey you, pea brain!" screeched the goose, angrily. "Answer my friend's question."

"Go bury your head!" replied the duck. By now all three ducks were giggling.

"Very strange bird," repeated Gloucester, who turned to the goose before adding "Any relation to you, is he?"

"Very distant. Very, very distant," the goose informed him, before attempting to talk to the ducks once more. "Come on lads, is there a river near here?"

"Christmas is coming! The goose is getting fat!" chanted the ducks, who then burst into laughter.

"Right, that does it," fumed the goose, who dived into the water and swam towards the hysterical ducks, grabbed the first one he came to by the neck, then dragged him back to the water's edge where he unceremoniously deposited him at Gloucester's feet. The duck squawked and flapped, as the goose pecked him hard about the head.

"I'm sorry," quacked the duck. "We were just having a bit of fun, that's all."

"A bit of fun!" screeched the goose. "Have you any idea who this is? Have you?" as he pecked the duck again.

"No Sir!" replied the duck, trying hard to avoid the blows.

"This," the goose informed him "is the great and brave Gloucester, who has in his time disarmed men with shotguns, single-handedly captured wild killer dogs, planned and taken part in daring escapes from certain death, that's who he is!" Upon hearing all of this Gloucester visibly blew up with pride and arrogance. "Yes I have," he said dreamily, lost in admiration of himself.

"So you had better answer his questions," continued the goose, "before he loses his temper, and that's not a pretty sight, I can tell you."

The duck looked up at Gloucester, in admiration and fear.

"Yes, yes," spluttered the duck "the river, er..mm.. let me think, yes, it's over there." He pointed with his beak. "About a day away."

"Only a day!" exclaimed a happy Gloucester.

"Yes Sir, as the duck flies, so to speak."

Gloucester's hopes were dashed as quickly as they had been raised.

"A day by air," he groaned "must be weeks on foot," and sat down, totally dejected, leaving the remainder of the interrogation to the goose.

"When were you last at the river?" he asked the duck.

"Two days ago," came the reply.

"Who else was there?"

"You know, other ducks, herons, swans, the usual things. Oh, and a raft."

"A raft!" exclaimed Gloucester, very interested in the duck's reply. "Did you see who was on it?"

"Er.. mm.. let me think," pondered the duck. "Ah yes, I remember now, because we all thought it was a bit odd. It's not every day you see a sheep and a goat on a raft, is it?"

"That's them!" cried Gloucester. "Cuddles and Nelly, they're still on the river."

"Well, so what?" butted in the goose, who couldn't understand why Gloucester had become so excited about the news of his friends. "We always knew that they were on the river, but I can't see how this duck's sighting of them is going to help us at all."

"Perhaps you can't, but I can," disagreed Gloucester. "If we could let them know that I'm all right, and that we're on our way to meet them, they could wait for us."

"And just how do you propose we do that?" demanded the goose, who thought Gloucester's suggestion was ridiculous.

"We're miles from the river, how on earth are we going

to get a message to them?"

"Simple! We ask this charming duck here to take it for us," he said, smiling broadly down at the duck.

"What, him!" exclaimed the goose, appalled at such an idea.

"Yes, why not?" argued Gloucester.

"I'll tell you why not," explained the goose. "All ducks are unreliable at the best of times, but this useless heap of feathers is worse than most. He's about as dependable as a bucket with a hole in it."

"Oh I'm sure you're wrong. He looks the most dependable of birds to me," replied Gloucester as he winked at the duck.

"Of course I am," agreed the duck, revelling in all the praise that was being heaped upon him.

"And you'll take the message then?" asked Gloucester in his most friendliest tone.

"Of course," replied the duck, getting to his feet, and who had suddenly become very fond of Gloucester. "I'll do it for you, Mister Gloucester, Sir, but not for him," and threw a cold stare in the direction of the goose.

"Splendid!" remarked Gloucester, "Now this is what I want you to do." He explained to the duck that he was to fly back to the river, find Cuddles and Nelly, tell them that he was all right, and on his way to meet them, and that they were not to travel any further down river until he had caught up with them. He went over it again, making sure that the duck had got the message right.

"Right, off you go then," Gloucester told him, once he was satisfied that the duck had fully understood what he had to do.

"We can't go now," remonstrated the duck.

"Why on earth not?" demanded Gloucester.

"Because it's late, and it's going to rain," explained the duck.

"But I thought ducks liked rain," added Gloucester.

"To splash about in, and swim around in, yes, but certainly not to fly in," the duck informed him. "But don't worry, we'll set out first thing tomorrow morning."

"Oh all right then," conceded Gloucester. "First thing tomorrow."

The duck swam quickly back to his friends and told them all what had been said.

"They won't do it," predicted the goose confidently to Gloucester, as they watched the three ducks discuss Gloucester's request. "It's a hopeless breed of bird is the duck."

The ducks returned to the side of the pond and addressed Gloucester: "We've talked it over and it's all agreed. We'll set off first thing in the morning to find your friends, and give them the message."

Gloucester thanked the ducks for their co-operation, and left them to continue their feeding. "There you are," he said to the goose. "All it takes is a little bit of civility, and you'll be amazed how kind some creatures can be."

"Hum," grunted the goose. "That's the last we'll see of them. By morning they'll have forgotten all about it."

"We'll see," Gloucester replied. "Let's get on. There are still a couple of daylight hours left. We should make the most of them."

The duck was certainly right about the rain. Gloucester and the goose had barely covered a mile when the skies darkened and the light began to fail.

"I think we'll call it a day," decided Gloucester, feeling the cold raindrops upon his skin. "Let's see if we can find somewhere to shelter for the night."

The goose was in full agreement, and they duly started looking for some suitable accommodation. After a few minutes they came upon a road. Since his capture, Gloucester had developed a great dislike of roads, and would only cross one when absolutely necessary. When they were confident that no-one was around, they quickly dashed across. By now the light had faded and the rain was falling much harder.

"There must be somewhere to shelter" complained Gloucester, who was starting to feel cold.

As they entered the field, the goose suddenly spotted a large boxlike shape in the gloom.

"Over there," he said, pointing toward the object, "that might be something."

They walked over to the shape, which turned out to be a large wicker basket lying on its side. Neither of them had ever seen a basket quite as large as this one. It was so big that there was space for both Gloucester and the goose to shelter in comfort, and there were even a couple of blankets inside, to wrap about themselves.

"This is all right," commented the goose, as he snuggled into his blanket.

"I wonder what it is?" muttered Gloucester, thoughtfully.

"I don't know, and I don't care," came the reply. After a few minutes the goose spoke again: "Gloucester, you know back there, when we were talking to those ducks?"

"Yes?" replied Gloucester, who was still mystified as to the purpose of such an enormous basket, and had been spending the past few minutes trying to work out what it could be used for.

"I hope you didn't mind me going on about you like I did, saying all those things about you disarming men, and capturing dogs and the like. I thought it might impress that stupid duck," the goose explained.

"Why should I mind?" replied Gloucester, failing to see what the goose was apologising for. "You only told the truth. I did do all those things, and more."

"Oh good," sighed the goose, sleepily. "I thought it might have embarrassed you."

"Of course not. I am, as you've probably noticed, by nature a modest sort of animal. But facts are facts, and although I wouldn't dream of boasting about such things myself, I see no harm in others telling of my great deeds of bravery to those who have lived less adventurous lives. I suppose one day there will be songs about me, monuments will be erected in my honour, sows will name their young after me, the weight of responsibility will weigh heavily on my shoulders. But you can be sure that I will carry on being my usual self: kind, modest and benevolent to those less fortunate than myself. Well, you wouldn't expect any less of me, would you?" He listened for a reply from the goose, but all he could hear was the rhythmic sounds of his breath as he slept. "Are you asleep?" Gloucester asked, but still failed to get a reply. "Typical!" Gloucester muttered to himself. "I don't know why I bother." But within a few minutes he himself was fast asleep.

* * * * *

The goose was woken early next morning by the sound of voices, human voices. He popped his head out of the basket to see what was going on, and decided to rouse Gloucester.

"Come on Gloucester, wake up," he said, pulling at the pig's ear.

"What is it?" asked Gloucester, drowsily.

"There are people outside, walking around in the field. Lots of people."

"The butcher?" asked Gloucester, who was now wide awake, and very concerned upon hearing the news.

"Don't think so," replied the goose, uncertainly.

Gloucester decided to take a look for himself. There were indeed a lot of people in the field, as the goose had said, all of whom seemed to be very busy, but neither Gloucester nor the goose could understand what they were doing. Some were carrying large cylindrical objects, which were obviously very heavy by the way people were struggling to carry them. At the same time another group of people were pulling what appeared to be a very large sheet across the ground, and stretching it out upon the ground."

What are they doing?" asked the very baffled goose.

"I really wouldn't know," admitted Gloucester. "Humans do the strangest things, but this is really odd." They retreated back into the safety of the basket, and tried to decide what was best to do next.

"Obviously they're not looking for us," reasoned Gloucester, "so I suggest that we lie low for the time being, wait until they finish whatever it is they're doing, and then slip away." The goose nodded in agreement.

After half-an-hour the goose decided to take another look at what was happening.

"Well?" asked Gloucester impatiently, as the goose drew his head back into the basket.

"It's all very odd. I just heard one man tell another one to "Fill her up!""

"Fill who up?" quizzed Gloucester.

"I really couldn't say," came the reply.

Then they heard a number of strange sounds, similar to air rushing through a tunnel, only different, and much louder.

"What is going on?" demanded Gloucester, who was beginning to get a bit annoyed at being stuck in the basket. The goose took another look, and in a soft whisper related what he could see back to Gloucester.

"I can see the people," he began, "The ones with the cylinder things, seem to be ... er.. mm ... how can I describe it, they're turning little taps on the cylinders, and somehow blowing air into that big sheet thing, which isn't really a sheet, but more like a great big sack, which is filling up with air, if you see what I mean?"

"It's about as clear as ditch water to me," growled Gloucester.

"As you said, humans do the strangest things," repeated the goose, returning to his seat.

They decided to do nothing for the moment, convinced that the people would soon get bored with putting air into a big sack, and go home. Boredom, as was the case with Gloucester and the goose, can soon lead to drowsiness and the two of them soon fell asleep, only to be rudely awakened an hour later.

For no apparent reason, to them that is, the basket in which they were hiding, suddenly tipped over, rolling its occupants to what was then its bottom. As Gloucester and the goose recovered their wits, and untangled themselves from the blankets which had wrapped around them, they saw that the opening by which they had entered was now pointing upwards, and that there was something very strange above it. The big bag, which the people were filling with air, was now somehow floating in the sky! All of a sudden they felt a lifting sensation for a little while, which thankfully came to an abrupt halt. Gloucester and the goose peered over the rim of the basket to see what had happened: to their amazement, the basket had actually lifted off the ground by at least a foot.

"What on earth?...." began Gloucester, who never bothered to finish his sentence.

They saw that the people were no longer interested in the big bag, and were busying themselves with some charts and papers.

"What do we do now?" squawked the goose. "I suggest we get out of here, but I'll need a rope or something to lower myself down. We're quite a way up and, if I was to jump, I could hurt myself." They both looked around for a suitable length of rope.

"Here!" pointed out the goose, "there's a bit of rope, tied to the side of the basket. I'll just untie it," and pulled on the rope with his beak. Unfortunately, the piece of rope in question was the rope anchoring the balloon to the ground.

"Got it!" cried the triumphant goose as he undid the

knot. Suddenly the balloon lurched upwards, now freed from its anchor.

"What have you done?" Gloucester bellowed at the goose.

"We appear to be going up," he sheepishly informed Gloucester. By then the people on the ground had noticed the balloon's ascent and rushed forward in the hope of bringing it under control but, sadly for them and for Gloucester, without success.

"What are we going to do now?" boomed Gloucester to the goose.

"I know what I'm going to do," the goose informed Gloucester. "I'm going to get out of here." He then hopped onto the rim of the basket and launched himself into the air, leaving a stunned Gloucester to watch his former companion glide slowly to the ground.

"I thought you said geese were loyal to their friends!" Gloucester shouted after him. The goose turned his head back towards Gloucester, shrugged his wings, and said, "Only to a point, old friend, and we've just reached that point. Goodbye! Gloucester, and good luck!"

Gloucester watched despairingly as the goose sailed effortlessly to the ground, then looked down at the people on the ground who were shouting up at him, shaking their fists. He watched with fascination as they grew smaller and smaller as he ascended into the sky, until they were no more than tiny dots, and the land lay beneath him like a patchwork quilt.

Confused, and more than a little afraid, he retreated to the relative safety of the basket and wrapped a blanket over him, having no desire to see any more. He sat there, his mind in a blank for quite some time, before summoning up enough courage to take another look.

Once again he peered over the rim at the land below: the scenery had changed. He was now passing over what appeared to be hills, but even they seemed to be hundreds of feet below him. By now he was less frightened, but no more the wiser as to how he was going to get down. Looking out onto the horizon, he saw three dots, heading his way. He watched them come closer until he could make out their shape. It was the ducks; they were taking his message to Nelly and Cuddles.

"I mustn't let them see I'm afraid," he told himself, and tried to mask his fear. As they drew nearer to the balloon, Gloucester called out to them. "Hello you lot!" he shouted, in a matter-of-fact manner. "I'm glad I spotted you." The ducks gasped in amazement at the sight that greeted them. "Slight change of plan," continued Gloucester casually. "I still want you to find my pals, but just tell them, that I'm on my way ... er ... this is the right way, isn't it?"

"Oh yes," gasped the duck, still stunned at the sight of the pig in a balloon.

"Thought it was," added Gloucester confidently, who then muttered to himself so that the ducks couldn't hear, "that's a bit of luck."

"How did you get into a balloon?" asked the astounded duck.

"I stole it," replied Gloucester, in an offhand manner.

"Gosh!" exclaimed the duck. "You really are as great as the goose said you were."

"It was nothing. I had to get to the river quickly, so I thought I'd take a ride in this thing."

"Can you fly it then?" asked one of the other ducks.

"Of course. Nothing to it really."

They all marvelled at the bravery, and cunning of this great pig before them.

"What happened to the goose?" asked the third duck.

"Oh him, he didn't fancy it, chickened out at the last minute, but we shouldn't be too hard on him," replied Gloucester. "You've either got it, or you haven't, courage that is. He just didn't have it, I'm sorry to say."

"Not like you, Mister Gloucester, Sir," quacked the

ducks. Gloucester merely shrugged his shoulders, in an attempt to feign modesty. "Well don't just flap around here, boys," rebuked Gloucester. "Go and find my pals and give them my message."

"Yes, Sir!" they quacked, "Right away, you can depend on us," and flew off with great urgency, leaving Gloucester to sink to the bottom of the basket, his act of bravado seeming to have completely exhausted him.

He remained in that position for at least another hour, still no further in solving the problem of how to get the balloon back down to earth, when a crow landed on the rim of the basket.

"Caw, caw," it croaked.

"Oh shut up!" said Gloucester crossly. The crow looked down at him, and ruffled his feathers. "Caw," he croaked again, "I've never seen a pig in a balloon before."

"Well you have now," replied Gloucester grumpily. "Now go away."

"Seen a dog once," continued the crow, ignoring Gloucester's remarks, "he was with two humans, but I've never seen a pig in a balloon before."

The crow's statement suddenly aroused Gloucester's curiosity. "You've seen these here balloons before have you?"

"Many times, in fact I've seen this very balloon on numerous occasions."

"You have!" exclaimed Gloucester, seeing a ray of hope at last.

"Normally there are two men in it," the crow informed Gloucester.

"And you've seen them fly it, actually fly the thing?" asked Gloucester very intensely.

"I really wouldn't call it flying: all they do is go up and float around for a while, and then go back down. It's not what you could honestly call flying, more like floating."

"All right, whatever it is they do, you've seen it?" demanded Gloucester.

The crow nodded, and tried to look very knowledgeable. "How do they do it?" Gloucester persisted.

"Gas," replied the crow.

"Gas?" queried Gloucester, puzzled by the reply.

"Yes, gas. They fill up the balloon with gas that is lighter than air, and when there's enough in it, the whole thing goes up."

This rather basic description of ballooning only succeeded in confusing Gloucester even further. He couldn't believe that anything could be lighter than air. A feather was light, but if you dropped it, it would float to the ground, and he couldn't think of anything lighter than a feather. Under normal circumstances he would have argued the point but, in his present predicament, he thought it best to accept what the crow had said to be correct.

"All right," admitted Gloucester, "we've established how this thing gets into the air, but how do we get it down?"

"Good question that," pondered the crow. "I haven't got a clue."

Gloucester groaned in dismay.

"I reckon you've got to let some gas out," continued the crow, ignoring Gloucester's groans. "That way the weight of the basket, with you in it, should drag you down ... I think!"

"Great!" enthused Gloucester. "How do we let the gas out?"

"How should I know?" croaked the crow. "Do I have to think of everything? You're the one travelling in the thing, you work it out. Try pulling some ropes and things."

Gloucester considered the crow's suggestion, and in light of the fact that in all the time he'd been stranded in the balloon he hadn't come up with one single idea, decided to act upon this advice. There were a number of ropes hanging down from the balloon, one of which he decided to pull. He took the rope in his teeth and gave it a tug ... nothing happened. He pulled again, only much harder this time. He felt something give, and heard the sound of air escaping from somewhere.

"Bravo!" exclaimed the crow. "You've done it."

"Yes, I have," confirmed Gloucester, feeling rather proud of himself as he felt the balloon start to descend. He looked down at the ground below, watching the fields beginning to get bigger ... in a hurry! "Er..mm.. we seem to be travelling a bit fast," observed Gloucester, who was becoming a little concerned as to their rate of descent. "How do we slow this thing down a bit?"

"Search me," replied the crow.

"What!" exclaimed Gloucester, now thrown into another panic. "If we don't slow down, we'll hit the ground at one heck of a speed."

"Looks that way," admitted the crow. "I'm off," and with that he took to the wing and flew out of the basket.

"Marvellous! Just marvellous!" Gloucester muttered to himself. "That's the last time I'm ever going to listen to anything covered in feathers. They're all the same: full of bright ideas, but at the first hint of trouble they're off like a shot. I'll never trust another bird as long as I live." He looked down at the ground rushing up to meet him, swallowed hard, before adding "as long as I live! What am I saying." He threw himself onto the bottom of the basket, curled up in a blanket, and waited for the inevitable crash!

## CHAPTER SIX : THE REUNION

Nelly and Cuddles had been so fascinated watching the balloon's swift descent, that they failed to notice the three ducks land nearby.

"Excuse me," said one of the ducks, as it clambered onto the raft, "Would your names be Nelly and Cuddles?" The two animals turned round to see who was addressing them.

"We are indeed," confirmed Cuddles, somewhat puzzled as to how the duck should know their names.

"Oh, I am glad we found you," continued the duck. "We've been looking up and down this river for over an hour."

"Really?" queried Nelly. "Why?"

"I've got a message from Mister Gloucester for you."

"What!" exclaimed Nelly and Cuddles in unison.

"Yes!" continued the duck. "He said for you not to worry, and he'll be with you soon."

"Will he indeed," remarked a bemused Cuddles.

"How?" The duck was about to reply, when one of the other ducks spotted the balloon.

"There he is now," he cried, looking up into the sky.

"Where?" asked Cuddles, following the duck's gaze.

"Up there, can't you see him?"

Cuddles once again stared into the sky, completely baffled at the duck's remarks. "The only thing that I can see is a balloo..." He failed to finish his sentence, turned to Nelly and said "You don't think ... it couldn't be ... no ... surely not."

A speechless Nelly looked at Cuddles, then at the ducks, and then at the balloon, with a stunned expression on her face.

"Ar-are you trying to tell me," stammered Cuddles, "that there is a large spotted pig, by the name of Gloucester, in that balloon?"

"Yes, Sir!" confirmed the duck proudly. "It's the great, and brave Gloucester."

"The great, and brave Gloucester!" exclaimed Cuddles, completely taken aback by Gloucester's newly acquired title.

"Isn't he going rather fast?" inquired Nelly, as they watched the balloon plummet to the earth.

"If you ask me," said Cuddles "it looks completely out of control. But with Gloucester in charge of it, you really wouldn't expect anything else."

The balloon passed quickly overhead and disappeared behind some trees where, a few seconds later, a crash could be clearly heard. Cuddles steered the raft to the river bank, where Nelly made it secure, before setting off in search of the balloon.

They quickly located the wreckage. It had landed in a tree, where the balloon had got tangled in the branches, leaving the basket suspended some twenty feet or so above the ground. They stood there looking up at it.

"I wonder if he's all right?" Nelly asked Cuddles, genuinely concerned.

Before Cuddles could reply, a loud groan could be heard coming from the basket, and a moment later a familiar face appeared over its rim.

"Behold, the flying pig!" cried Cuddles, in good humour, relieved to see that his troublesome friend was none the worse for the crash. Gloucester looked down to see his old friends, and as he did so his dazed face suddenly lit up into the biggest smile imaginable.

"Nelly ! Cuddles!" he yelled with joy. "Is it really you?"

"The very same," confirmed a very happy Nelly.

"Am I glad to see you two," said Gloucester wearily. "You've no idea what I've been through."

"Well you can tell us all about it later," Cuddles told him. "But first, how do you propose to get down from there?"

"I haven't given it much thought really," admitted Gloucester. Just then a loud ripping sound could be heard, as the fabric of the balloon started to tear in the branches of the tree. Suddenly the basket, no longer supported from above, gave way and fell to the floor with a bang, tipping Gloucester onto the ground. By now the ducks had arrived on the scene, and upon seeing their hero lying on the grass, dashed over to his aid.

"Are you all right?" asked one, very concerned, as the others fussed over him.

"I'm fine boys, really, I'm all right," he assured the ducks.

"Isn't he marvellous?" commented one of the ducks to Nelly and Cuddles, who were watching the whole proceedings with complete astonishment.

"I could describe Gloucester in many ways, but 'marvellous' would not be one of them," Cuddles muttered to Nelly. Gloucester staggered to his feet, still with the ducks fussing over him.

"Hurray for the great and brave Gloucester!" they chanted, again and again.

"I think I'm going to be sick," said Cuddles, to no-one in particular. After Gloucester had completely regained his senses, the three animals sat down in the shade of a tree where Gloucester recounted his adventures since his disappearance. Nelly and Cuddles listened with interest, and at times disbelief, to his tale. Obviously Gloucester's account of what had happened to him wasn't entirely accurate: according to him, at no time had he been afraid, and the taking of the balloon was planned and quite intentional. But both Nelly and Cuddles knew him well enough to take some of what he said as pure exaggeration.

"You've certainly had an adventure," admitted Nelly, when Gloucester had finished his tale.

"You must have been a little bit frightened at times?" asked Cuddles, sceptically.

"No," replied the pig confidently.

"Not even when you were in the balloon, all that way up?" added Nelly. "I'm sure I would have been terrified."

"No, I had everything under control."

"You didn't appear to be under control when you came down," Cuddles noted.

Gloucester gave the sheep a hard stare, before replying. "A slight miscalculation, that's all it was. I was doing fine until then."

Cuddles merely said, "Oh!" and winked at Nelly, who fought back a giggle. "Correct me if I'm wrong," continued Cuddles, "but I don't think you mentioned how much you made at auction?"

Gloucester fell silent, which was very unusual for Gloucester.

"Yes, how much did you sell for?" enquired Nelly, genuinely interested.

"I'm not saying," replied Gloucester, huffily. "Mind your own business."

"Come on Gloucester, you can tell us, we're your friends," persisted Cuddles.

"I'm not telling you!" he informed them, in a very adamant tone. "Now if you don't mind, I'd like to go and see the raft," and with that he rose to his feet and headed for the river, leaving Cuddles and Nelly still sitting under the tree.

"I don't think he made very much," laughed Cuddles, as he watched Gloucester walk away.

"You could be right," added Nelly, who had also begun to giggle.

"Couldn't have done," continued Cuddles, "otherwise he would have told us. You know him as well as I do; if he'd sold for a lot of money, he couldn't resist telling us how much he's worth."

They jumped to their feet and raced after Gloucester, pestering him to tell them how much he'd made. But Gloucester would not tell, and never did. In Gloucester's opinion there are some insults far too cruel to ever be shared, even with the closest of friends.

* * * * *

The three companions continued their journey reunited. Even Cuddles had to admit that it was good to have their old friend back again.

"Let's face it," he told Nelly on one occasion, "It was a bit boring when he wasn't around, but now he's back things are bound to liven up a bit, disaster follows him around like a shadow."

"You can be cruel at times," Nelly scolded Cuddles.

"Perhaps," commented Cuddles, "but it's true."

A couple of days after the reunion the weather changed from the glorious summer's sun to rain. The skies turned grey, the rain poured down, making the river swell and increase in speed to the extent that travelling upon it became both dangerous and unwise.

"It's no good," conceded Cuddles one morning as they

stared at the grey angry waters roaring past them. "We'll have to tie up for a while until the rain stops and the river returns to normal."

"It would be the safest thing to do," agreed Nelly. "With all this rain running off the land, the river has risen at least two feet."

"Not to mention all the hazards that have been washed into it," added Gloucester, as he watched another uprooted tree being swept along in the water. They made sure that the raft was firmly secured to a solid looking oak tree before considering what they were going to do about shelter for the next few days, until the river returned to its old friendly self.

The ducks or, as Cuddles has christened them, 'Gloucester's Fan Club', had decided to travel with the animals for the time being, mainly because they wanted to hear more wonderful tales of adventure from Gloucester who, in turn, was more than willing to oblige them. The weather, however, and the conditions on the river persuaded them to return to their pond. The three animals bade them farewell, much to Cuddles's relief, as he had had to endure what he considered to be hours of agony while Gloucester related even more tales of his bravery.

The three companions set off across the muddy fields in search of shelter. After a couple of hours, cold and thoroughly wet through, they came upon a deserted farm. They approached the farm with great caution, just in case there were any humans still present. A quick reconnoitre however soon confirmed their original impressions: the farm was uninhabited. Upon closer inspection they could see that the farm was quite run down, and had obviously not been lived in for a number of years.

"Got a good roof," observed Nelly, as she stared at the farmhouse. "That's important."

"Oh yes," agreed Gloucester. "At least we'll be able to stay dry."

"The farm buildings look a bit of a mess," Cuddles pointed out, surveying the dilapidated range of farm buildings, before adding, "I suggest we stay in the house itself."

All were in agreement and set about finding a way of entering the house. At first glance, it appeared that the premises were very secure, and there seemed no way of gaining entry: all the doors were locked and the windows secured. They walked around the house a number of times, trying to find a way in, but there was none.

"There's nothing for it," declared Cuddles, "we'll have to break the door down."

"Sounds a bit drastic to me," remarked Nelly, who had never been a great believer in brute force and ignorance. Gloucester on the other hand was in total agreement with Cuddles.

"Right!" enthused Cuddles. "Let's have a go at the front door."

Gloucester and Cuddles examined the door, deciding on how to approach the problem. They both agreed to charge the door head on at the same time convinced, in their opinion, that the door would surely give way under their combined weight. They measured their run and charged, hitting the door at full speed. It shook a little but didn't give an inch, leaving the two animals in an untidy heap on the floor, dazed.

"So much for the strong arm tactics," chuckled Nelly, who then proceeded to find another less violent way of entry. Once again she walked slowly around the house, carefully examining all the doors and windows in the chance that they had missed something earlier, when she heard another crash as her two colleagues once more attempted to beat the door down.

"I do wonder about those two sometimes," she said to herself wistfully. While examining the back of the house she spotted an old trap door at the base of the house, and on

closer examination she noticed an old iron ring, which was attached to the door. Nelly nimbly slid one of her horns through the ring and pulled, opening the door, to reveal a flight of steps, leading into the cellar. She considered telling the others about her find, when she heard yet another crash at the front door, and took the view that by now both Gloucester and Cuddles would probably be in bad moods, so she decided to leave them to it.

Nelly followed the steps down into the cellar which, although quite dark, had sufficient light from the open trap door for her to see where she was going. On the other side of the cellar, she found another flight of steps, which led upwards, out of the cellar, into what had once been the hallway. From where she was standing Nelly could see the front door, which suddenly shook violently as Cuddles and Gloucester once more hurled themselves at it from the other side. She trotted over to the door to see that it was secured by two heavy bolts, one on the top and one on the bottom. Cuddles and Gloucester could be heard arguing on the other side of the door. Nelly stood up on her hind legs in an attempt to reach the top bolt. She could just touch it with the tip of her nose, although rusty, and a little stiff, she just managed to slide it back. The bottom bolt proved to be much easier to move and she soon had the door free from all restrictions. Then, just as she was about to open the door, Cuddles and Gloucester decided to charge. The door, no longer bolted, flew open, and Nelly saw her two friends charge past her across the hall, through the door at the other end, and disappear at speed down the flight of steps that led into the cellar, whereupon she heard a loud crash.

Although Nelly would always remember this incident with great amusement in the future, at the time she was quite concerned that they may have hurt themselves. She quickly dashed over to the doorway and looked down to see Cuddles and Gloucester in a heap at the bottom of the steps, groaning, but none the worse for their accident. Nelly, relieved that no serious injuries had been inflicted, began to laugh as the other two scrambled to their feet.

"I fail to see what's so funny," stated Gloucester, addressing the hysterical goat, "we could have hurt ourselves."

"What happened?" groaned Cuddles, who was a little more dazed than his companion, shook his head, looked to see where he was, and then remarked to Gloucester triumphantly: "There you are, I told you one more bang would do it."

"Oh shut up!" rebuked Gloucester crossly, realising what a fool he had made of himself.

Upon examination they found that the house, although having been empty for so long, was in remarkably good condition. There was a little damp on the walls and the whole place smelt a little musty but, all in all, it seemed as good a place as any to weather out the storm. With it being uninhabited there was no furniture in any of the rooms and nothing for the animals to make any sort of bed, so it was decided to investigate the outbuildings in the hope of finding some suitable bedding material.

The buildings were, as Cuddles had previously observed, in a rundown condition. Half the roof was missing, stable doors hung off their hinges, and nearly all the loft floors were rotten and far too dangerous to walk on. They searched through each stable and loose box, looking for bedding. The smell of neglect and decay seemed to hang over the place. Gloucester found some old sacks that he thought might serve his purpose but on closer inspection, found them to be rotten. At one doorway, Cuddles stopped abruptly. Nelly who was also with him, asked him what was wrong.

"I can smell dogs," replied Cuddles tersely, as he sniffed the air. "There's been a dog here recently."

Nelly, who had never forgotten her experiences with dogs in the past, felt a shiver run down her spine. "Is he still there?" she asked nervously, not daring to look herself.

Cuddles walked bravely into the loose box, and looked around.

"No-one here now!" he called out to Nelly, who was greatly relieved to hear the news. She promptly joined Cuddles who was looking at some chicken feathers on the floor.

"There's definitely been a dog in here," confirmed Cuddles, "and these feathers are all that's left of his last meal." They both stared at the feathers with an uneasy silence, neither daring to say what each was thinking.

Suddenly their attention was diverted by a noise in the loft above them. They looked up to see a pair of yellow eyes looking down at them from out of the gloom. Nelly suddenly felt very frightened, and even Cuddles felt very uneasy at the sight of the eyes watching them.

"Is that you Gloucester?" asked Cuddles uncertainly. There was no reply.

They stared at the eyes, which in turn stared back at them. Because of the dullness of the day and the omission of light in the loft, it was too dark for either of the animals to guess at the size or shape of the animal looking down at them, all of which made for an unnerving situation.

"Gloucester, if this is your idea of a joke, I can assure you it's in very poor taste," grumbled Cuddles, who for once rather hoped that it might be the pig playing the fool. Still there was no reply. Only the eyes that gazed down, unblinking. Finally, and thankfully, a voice came from the direction of the eyes.

"Are you friendly?" it asked, in a low purring tone.

"We're very friendly," sighed Nelly, who was greatly relieved to find that the creature in the loft was more afraid of them than they were of it.

"If I come down, you promise not to chase me?" it asked in a long drawling tone.

"Of course not!" answered Cuddles, somewhat surprised

at the question. Then, from out of the gloom of the loft, a large black and white cat jumped down to join them. Nelly and Cuddles introduced themselves to the cat, who was called Robbie, by which time Gloucester had joined them.

"You seemed very nervous before?" observed Nelly.

"I thought it might be that dog come back," replied Robbie, licking a paw. "He chased me all over the farm. I've been hiding in that loft since yesterday." The news that what Cuddles had earlier suspected was correct, unnerved all present.

"This dog, did you get a good look at him?" asked Nelly seriously.

"I should say so. He nearly caught me once, and would have done, if I hadn't hidden in that loft."

"Well, what did he look like?" demanded Cuddles, fearing the worst.

"That, I can easily tell you. I'll never forget him as long as I live. A large brute of a thing, black as night, with a nasty looking scar running down his face."

The news that their old adversary, Scar, was in the neighbourhood, brought a veil of silence over the three companions, though none was in any doubt what the others were thinking. It was Cuddles, who probably received the news with a mixture of emotions and who, as usual, finally broke the silence.

"When did all this happen?" he asked the cat.

"Two days ago. After he found he couldn't catch me, he wandered off, only to return later that night with a hen from the local poultry farm, the remains of which you've seen." The three animals nodded in recognition of the fact. "He then slept in this very box that night, and left early yesterday morning. I've been up here ever since, in case he was to turn up again. I didn't fancy meeting him out in the open."

"I can understand that!" sympathised Nelly, before turning to Cuddles. "What do you suggest we do?"

"Just because he was here yesterday, doesn't necessarily mean he's going to come back," reasoned Cuddles. "If he follows his usual habits, he'll be long gone by now, in case the poultry farmer is looking for him."

"On the other hand, he might return at any moment," remarked Nelly, pessimistically.

"I don't see why we're worrying so much," commented Gloucester. "After all, there are three of us. I can't see Scar tackling us all at the same time. All we have to do is stick together and, as for the nights, we'll be in the house where we can bolt the door. He'll never get in there." The other animals were inclined to agree with Gloucester, to a point.

"The thing is, Gloucester," explained Nelly, "you've never actually met Scar. You can't imagine what he's like. He's ... he's ..."

"Vicious?" suggested the cat.

"Evil, might be nearer the mark," corrected Cuddles.

"Well, whatever he is," continued Gloucester, "he's still only a dog, on his own, and there are three of us."

"Four!" added the cat. "If there is any chance of you three getting him into a corner, I want to dig my claws into him," and with that he swiped the air with his paw, displaying his razor sharp claws in mock battle.

They all agreed to keep together during their stay at the farm, and that under no circumstances was anyone to wander off alone. Bolting the door of the house at night, and securing the trap door which Nelly had found, would ensure the house would be a safe haven during the hours of darkness. Robbie, the cat, asked if he could sleep in the house with them rather than risk staying in the outbuildings, where he felt very vulnerable. The three companions readily agreed.

After further exploration, the three animals found some hay and straw which would serve as bedding, and moved it into the house. The cat also showed them an old garden which, although neglected for a number of years, still boasted a number of fruit trees. Upon closer inspection Nelly found, to her delight, that there was a good supply of apple leaves. While in another corner, a few old potato sets had been left to grow wild, a fact that did not escape Gloucester's attention, and he soon started to root them up with his nose. Meanwhile Cuddles enjoyed the clover that grew in abundance everywhere. That night they all retired to the safety of the house, bolted the door, and rested on their soft beds.

"How long have you lived here?" Nelly asked the cat.

"A long time," replied Robbie, thoughtfully. "In fact, all my life. I was born here. It was much different then: a proper farm, with kind people who lived in the house, and fed us every morning. There were cows in the sheds, hens and turkeys. It was a very busy farm when I was a kitten, not like now, all neglected." There was a hint of sadness in his voice.

"What happened then? Where did the people go?" asked Cuddles, finding it a little strange that such a nice farm should be left to go derelict.

"I don't know where they went," replied Robbie. "It all happened so quickly. I remember sitting in the kitchen with my brothers and sisters one morning, having just been fed some bread and milk. I heard the farmer tell his wife something about selling up, something to do with an overdraft, whatever one of those is, and that they couldn't go on. I was only a kitten and didn't really understand it all and, to be honest, I still don't. But I know the farmer and his wife were very unhappy about it all. Anyway, a couple of weeks later a lot of people came and held something called an auction, and everything was taken: all the cows and hens, all the machinery, and the furniture out of the house. It all went, and the farmer and his wife went as well. All the cats were sorry to see them go. They were very kind to us, and all the animals, but I don't think they wanted to go because the farmer's wife was crying when she left."

All the animals found Robbie's story a very sad tale, especially Gloucester who, having suffered the ordeal of an auction himself, was better placed than most to appreciate the seriousness of it all.

"So why is it you stayed on?" enquired Cuddles.

"The day after the sale," continued the cat "some people out of the village came for the cats, to give them good homes, but I was determined to stay here and hid away in one of the lofts, refusing all the food which was offered to me, knowing full well that someone would grab me. I had no intention of leaving the farm. I was born here. It's my home."

"It must be lonely," commented Nelly. "Who looks after you?"

"I get by," purred the cat very independently. "There are plenty of rats and mice around, and the occasional sparrow, and I get plenty of visitors or I'll visit neighbouring farms. There's even one old lady, who I stay with in the winter if the weather gets too bad, who'll feed me. So you see, I have quite a good time of it."

The three animals then explained to Robbie the reason for their journey and the intended destination, with an account of their own adventures to date. Gloucester, of course, went into great detail regarding his own exploits, and kept everyone up half the night. Naturally, when the subject of how much Gloucester had made at auction was raised, the pig refused to answer the question, despite a lot of prompting by the others, much to the amusement of the remaining company.

CHAPTER SEVEN : SCAR

As the three animals slept in the safety of the house, a dark sinister figure prowled the river bank. For nearly three weeks, Scar had scoured the country in an attempt to find Nelly and exact his revenge. His injuries had prevented him from following the raft, but now his wounds had healed and he was as fit and strong as ever. A lifetime's experience of the countryside, and his knowledge of its highways and byways had meant that he could take short cuts across country, to ensure that sooner or later he would catch up with the goat.

He sniffed the raft moored alongside the river bank and instantly recognised Nelly's scent. He smiled cruelly to himself as he realised that he had finally tracked her down. Although he had no way of knowing where the three companions were staying, he correctly assumed that it would only be a question of time before they returned to the raft. He would wait. Patience, he had found, nearly always paid off.

\* \* \* \* \*

After three days, the rain stopped and the sun shone once again. The three companions decided to go down to the river and check that all was well with the raft. The fields were saturated with all the rain that had fallen over the past few days, and the animals' feet squelched in the mud as they walked. Ditches, unable to take all the water away, were overflowing onto the fields, causing small ponds to form upon the land. Robbie had declined the invitation to go with them; like all cats, he hated the wet, and the idea of getting his paws wet appalled him.

"I think that cat had the right idea," commented Cuddles, as he pulled his feet out of the mud.

"What!" retorted Gloucester, "You must be joking! This

is marvellous!" By now the pig had rolled around in the muddier parts of the field and was plastered from head to toe in a brown gooey mess. "Great for the skin, this stuff," he informed his friends, who were quite prepared to take his word for it, without actually trying it.

Upon reaching the raft, they were all relieved to see that it was still there and had suffered no ill effects. The river, on the other hand, was still far too dangerous to even consider attempting the resumption of their journey.

"Perhaps tomorrow," remarked a disappointed Nelly, who was very keen to put as much distance between themselves and the last sighting of Scar as soon as possible.

"I doubt it," mused Cuddles, as he watched the grey angry waters rush past them. "There is still a lot of water on the fields which has to drain off. I'm sorry to say it may be at least a couple of days before the river returns to normal."

Nelly, who for no apparent reason, suddenly felt uncomfortable, suggested that they all return to the safety of the house, and started to make her way back.

"That's strange," commented Gloucester, who was looking down at the muddy ground near the raft.

"What's strange?" asked Cuddles, joining his friend's side.

"These footprints. They look like a fox's, only they seem too large," continued Gloucester as he examined the prints. Cuddles suddenly felt a cold shiver run through his body as he realised who had made the prints. Gloucester, too, suddenly became aware of the significance of his discovery, and looked at Cuddles. Neither said a word, but turned to check where Nelly was. She was by now a good fifty yards ahead of them, walking along the river bank, lost in her thoughts.

Cuddles bellowed after her, "Nelly! Wait for us."

Cuddles and Gloucester immediately raced off after her, concerned that she should not be left alone for a moment longer. Then, to their horror, they saw Scar suddenly leap out of the undergrowth and pounce on Nelly, sinking his teeth hard into the top of her head. It was like some terrible nightmare. As they ran towards her, it was clear that Scar was trying to drag his victim to the floor, where he could grab for her throat, which would mean certain death for her. Despite the fact that the dog was savaging her ear, and pulling with all his might at the same time, Nelly instinctively made every effort to remain on her feet, although it would only be a question of time before Scar's superior strength would win him the day.

Fortunately it didn't take Cuddles long to reach his stricken friend, and he promptly butted Scar in the ribs with his hard head, sending the dog sprawling to the ground.

Without thought or hesitation, Cuddles attempted to make the most of his advantage, and tried to get another crushing blow in before Scar had a chance to get to his feet. His charge missed by inches, as the agile dog managed to scramble out of the way just in time.

"Get out of here," growled Scar, who stared at Cuddles. "I've no quarrel with you. Why get yourself hurt, defending this goat?" To Scar, terms such as loyalty and friendship meant nothing, and he couldn't understand why one animal would risk injury to protect another.

"You murdering Devil!" rasped Cuddles. "You killed my mother!" He then lowered his head, and charged. Once more Scar nimbly sidestepped the oncoming ram, and bit him on the back of the neck as he rushed past. Fortunately Cuddles had a good growth of wool which protected him from any serious injury, but the weight of the dog caused him to lose his balance and trip over. They rolled over together, locked in combat, with Scar still holding onto Cuddles' wool, not prepared to lose his advantage. Both were too preoccupied to even care about anything else, but Nelly and Gloucester could clearly see that they were rolling dangerously close to the water's edge. Unable to prevent it, they watched, helpless, as the two adversaries toppled into the river and disappeared beneath the grey angry waters! For what seemed an agonising length of time, neither Nelly nor Gloucester could see anything of them. Finally they emerged in the middle of the river, some feet apart, gasping for breath, and vainly struggling against the fast flowing current which dragged them along. Nelly, despite her injuries, quickly realised the danger that Cuddles was in as he disappeared once more beneath the water.

"Quick!" she urged Gloucester "Get the raft free. We must save Cuddles before he drowns."

Gloucester quickly untied the raft, and they leapt on board. The speed of the river soon had them racing towards their stricken friend. Gloucester, who was operating the tiller, found the craft very difficult to handle in the turbulent waters and had to fight the river every inch of the way, while Nelly, who was standing at the front of the raft, kept an eye on Cuddles, who was getting into more difficulties. By now his wool, saturated with water, was beginning to drag him

down. Despite his great strength, he found it impossible to resist the awesome force of the river and gradually he felt himself become weaker and weaker: it would only be a question of time before exhaustion overcame him, and the raging river would claim yet another victim!

The raft, under Gloucester's guidance, reached him just in time, and Nelly urged Cuddles to save himself. With his last dregs of strength he managed to lift his front feet onto the raft, and hold on. Gloucester, seeing that Cuddles was in part safe from any immediate danger, informed the others that the raft was out of control as it careered down the river.

"It's all I can do to stop it tipping over!" he shouted at the top of his voice, as he struggled with the tiller.

"Head for the river bank!" Nelly yelled back in reply. She was unable to lend a hand, as she was holding onto Cuddles' legs, in case he slipped back into the river.

Gloucester leaned hard against the tiller in an attempt to steer to safety. At first all his efforts were in vain, as the force of the river seemed to override the rudder, but gradually he felt the raft respond. Gloucester was quite aware that they were travelling far too fast and that when they finally reached the river bank, there would be a crash, but at the time it seemed the better of two evils. He was perfectly aware that Cuddles, even with Nelly's help, could not hold on much longer, and that if he should slip back into the water he would certainly drown. All that mattered was that they reach the safety of the bank as quickly as possible.

As they neared the water's edge, Gloucester urged the others to hold on. They hit the bank with a shuddering thud that sent both Nelly and Gloucester sprawling to the floor. Quickly they regained their feet and hurried to help Cuddles, who was near to exhaustion. Luckily the water where they had landed was not too deep and the two animals could wade in to assist their stricken friend. Cuddles' normal weight was considerable, but combined with all the water which was being retained in his wool, and the fact that he was now terribly weak, both Nelly and Gloucester found that getting him out of the water was no easy matter. Nevertheless, after much pulling and shoving, they finally managed to wrestle him to the bank and the safety of dry ground. Their exertions left all concerned completely drained of strength and they collapsed in a heap.

The raft on the other hand did not come through the experience well, and the crash had inflicted a lot of damage. One of the oil drums, which had made contact with the bank first, was buckled and was letting water in; a number of the boards were cracked and splintered, and the rope which held everything together had snapped in a number of places. As the three companions lay there trying to catch their breath, they watched with horror as the raft began to break up in the rough waters, helpless to do anything about it and too tired to even try. All they could do was watch as bits of wood and tyres and the three remaining barrels parted company and floated down the river. Despair hit them hard: their old trusty raft gone. No-one said a word. It wasn't anyone's fault; it was just one of those things.

The little group of animals on the river bank made for a forlorn and depressing spectacle. Cuddles, who had swallowed a great deal of water, was coughing and spluttering for breath, while Nelly was bleeding badly from the ear which Scar had savaged, and the blood trickled down the side of her face.

"Curse that dog!" muttered Gloucester, as he inspected Nelly's ear which had almost been torn in two.

"Scar!" exclaimed Nelly, who had almost forgotten about the dog in all the excitement. "What's happened to him?"

"Drowned, I should imagine," replied Gloucester hopefully. "I can't see how he could have escaped the river on his own." They gazed out onto the river and saw, to their dismay and disbelief, the dog drag himself out of the water onto the opposite bank. "How on earth did he survive that!" remarked an amazed Gloucester. "I saw him go under."

"Perhaps it's true what Cuddles said, about the Devil himself looking after him," mumbled Nelly thoughtfully.

When Cuddles had recovered sufficiently, they told him that Scar had not perished in the river, and that he was on the opposite river bank. Cuddles took the news badly. He would have gladly given his own life if it had meant an end for the savage dog.

"What are we going to do now?" asked Nelly, realising how bad their position was. "With the raft gone, there's no way we can escape him."

"We're all right for the moment," assured Cuddles. "With the river being as it is, there's no chance of him crossing it."

"But what happens when the river returns to normal? He could swim over then," reasoned a very concerned Nelly.

"Or if we came to a bridge," added Gloucester thoughtfully. Neither of the other two animals had even considered this possibility but, now that it had been brought to their attention, they greeted the prospect with some trepidation.

"Would he really attack us now?" asked Nelly, trying to find some glimmer of hope. "Now we know he's about? As Gloucester said, there are three of us. Not even Scar would attack us all at once."

"He wouldn't attack us all at once," Cuddles reliably informed them, "he'd wait until one of us was alone, or wait for night and pounce when we were asleep."

"We could keep watch," suggested Nelly, after a long, uneasy silence. "One stays awake, while the others sleep. That way someone would always be on the lookout for him."

Cuddles realised that, although Nelly's idea had some merit, the chances of it working indefinitely were slim. Eventually one of them would fall asleep while on guard, and Scar would only need one chance. However, seeing how concerned Nelly was about the whole situation, he didn't expose the flaws in her plan but congratulated her on a marvellous idea. He assured her that if the day came when

Scar was on the same side of the river as themselves, they would certainly put her plan into action, although in his own mind he had resolved that Scar must not cross the river, at any cost.

By mid-afternoon Cuddles had fully recovered from his ordeal in the river, and they decided to move off. In light of the fact that they had lost the raft, they were left with no alternative but to continue their journey on foot. As they walked, they saw Scar, on the opposite bank, rise to his feet and walk in the same direction as themselves, always keeping pace.

By the time evening arrived, the sun had dried out Cuddles' wool, and Nelly's ear had stopped bleeding. She had also washed the blood off her hair in the river. The ear itself looked raw and painful, and throbbed continuously, but Nelly herself put on a brave face and assured the others that it looked a lot worse than it really was, although in truth she was in terrible pain.

As they settled down for the night, they could just see Scar, in the failing light, also stopping to rest. His progress on the opposite bank had been a constant reminder of what might happen when he had an opportunity to cross over to their side of the river. It soon became dark but, despite the fact that all the animals were tired, sleep would not come easily to any of them. Cuddles then had an idea.

"Look you two," he whispered, so as not to attract the dog's attention. "I suggest we carry on while it's dark, and put as many miles between ourselves and Scar as possible." All were agreeable and set off once more. The journey in the dark was a solemn affair, with very few words being exchanged; but by the time morning broke, they considered that they had travelled a good number of miles. As the sun rose in the east and the dawn chorus commenced, they sank to the ground, exhausted, and were soon fast asleep.

It must have been midday before they awoke. Nelly, being the first to rise, she stretched, yawned, and gazed out over the river, only to see something which made her blood run cold. There, on the opposite bank, was Scar, just sitting looking back at her! She quickly roused the others and broke the news to them.

"How?" was all Cuddles could utter.

"I don't know," shrugged Nelly, who was as puzzled as anyone as to how Scar could have travelled so far in such a short time, and known exactly where they had stopped.

"There's something unnatural about that dog," declared Gloucester, as he stared over to where their tormentor was sitting. Cuddles was obviously very disappointed that his plan to give Scar the slip had failed so miserably.

"Why don't we leave the river and head inland," suggested Nelly, "while the river is still up and stopping him from crossing over?"

"The only problem is," replied Cuddles logically, "that if we do that, Scar will eventually cross over, perhaps tomorrow, or the day after. Whenever, he'll come looking for us, except we won't know when. We'll be forever looking over our shoulders wondering where he is. No, it's best we stay with the river, where we can keep an eye on him, wait for him to make his move and deal with him then."

Obviously Nelly didn't relish the thought of crossing swords with Scar again but, after due consideration, realised that Cuddles was right.

"When the time comes," continued Cuddles, "we must finish the job. I don't agree with taking another animal's life but, in this instance, Scar has left us no choice. He's made it quite clear, it's him or us. We must be prepared to do whatever is necessary to protect ourselves."

* * * * *

The next three days wore very heavy on the animals' nerves. The constant presence of Scar was always there to haunt them, and also as a reminder of the eventual conflict that had to take place before this most unhappy situation could be resolved.

On the morning of the fourth day of their ordeal, the animals rose to find Scar as usual waiting for them on the other side of the river. He was sitting down chewing on something.

"Looks like he went hunting last night," commented Gloucester. "I wonder what he's eating?"

"Probably some poor defenceless creature," answered Cuddles, unable to see clearly exactly what it was that Scar had caught during the night.

Nelly, who was considered to have the best eyesight of the three, strained to see.

"It looks like," she informed the others, "he's chewing on a very large bone."

"He must have made a big kill last night," commented Cuddles, who shuddered with repulsion at the thought of it. None of the animals needed any encouragement to move on and leave the gruesome scene behind them.

By mid-morning they reached a bend in the river, and as they rounded it they saw something they had all been dreading: a bridge! This surely would be Scar's chance to cross over onto their side.

"Quick!" urged Cuddles, "Get to the bridge, before he has a chance to use it." They raced towards the bridge, without saying a word. On many occasions they had planned what to do if and when a situation like this presented itself, and each knew what was expected of him.

Fortunately, the three companions reached the bridge first and took up their positions, with Gloucester in the middle and Nelly and Cuddles either side of him. Together they formed a barricade across the bridge which they hoped would stop the menacing dog. The bridge itself was the old sandstone type, much seen in the country and built many years ago. There they waited in trepidation for Scar. Although time seemed to drag on painfully slowly, it was only a few minutes before Scar's ugly features appeared before them. He paused, somewhat surprised that the three animals should be there to meet him.

"What's all this then," he snarled sarcastically. "One last defiant gesture before the end?"

"You're not crossing this bridge, Scar," Cuddles told him sternly.

"Be off with you," added Gloucester, "or we'll throw you into the river."

Scar laughed cruelly. "Very brave, aren't you. But tell me, how brave will you be when I pick you off one by one."

The three animals stared at their tormentor, wondering what to do next. It was quite obvious that he had no intention of going away. As they stood on the bridge, deadlocked, engrossed in their own dilemmas, no-one noticed another animal which was approaching the bridge from Scar's side of the river. It was a large Hereford bull. He walked powerfully onto the bridge, and roared. Such was the loudness of his roar that it made all the animals jump, even Scar.

"You! You're the one!" he bellowed at Scar. "You're the one I've been looking for, you murdering devil!" and shook his massive head, complete with horns, at him. Scar suddenly found himself trapped on the bridge, blocked at one end by the three companions and at the other by the enraged bull. Thinking that he had more chance of getting past the three companions than the bull, he made a dash for that end. As he approached, Nelly shook her own horns at him, while Gloucester opened his mouth to display a row of sharp looking teeth, and Cuddles lowered his head ready to inflict a crushing blow. Scar, upon seeing that he had little chance of getting past the animals without injury, turned back and decided to try his luck against the bull; after all, there was only one animal to avoid at that end of the bridge.

For such a large, heavy animal the bull moved remarkably quickly. Scar had nearly slipped past him, when the bull swung his heavy head towards him, catching the dog with one of his horns, trapping him against the wall of the bridge with his head. Scar screamed in agony as the bull pushed hard, bringing all his colossal strength to bear. Later Gloucester swore he could hear the dog's ribs crack. The bull backed off, and Scar staggered from the wall back into the middle of the bridge, with blood trickling from his nose and mouth. Cuddles, seeing his opportunity, dashed forward and butted the stricken dog hard in his already damaged ribs, sending him sprawling towards the bull, who once more roared and sent his hard broad head crashing down on top of him!

The animals slowly congregated around the dog, which lay limp on the bridge.

"Is he dead?" asked Nelly. "Is he finally dead?"

"Yes," confirmed Cuddles, "he's dead." There was no remorse in his voice, or elation, only relief.

"Are you sure?" enquired Gloucester. "We don't want any mistakes this time." The bull picked up Scar's broken body on his horns, and tossed it into the river where it was soon swallowed up in the murky waters.

"He's dead now," remarked the bull, as they watched the spot where Scar had disappeared. "He'll take no more of my calves."

Nelly remembered what Scar had been eating earlier that morning. He must have killed a calf from this bull's herd the night before, and the bull had tracked him down to exact his own revenge. She also remembered something she had heard long ago; a saying which seemed very appropriate for this moment. "He who lives by the sword, must die by the sword."

After a while the bull calmed down, and the three companions found him to be a pleasant, agreeable type of chap, despite the ferocity he had shown in dealing with Scar.

Their suspicions about Scar having taken one of his calves the previous night were quite correct.

"Daisy, the mother of the calf, is very upset," he explained to the others. "The little calf was only two days old. I know killing the brute can't bring the calf back, but at least it's stopped him from ever doing it again. I must add that your help was invaluable in stopping him from escaping. Why did you do it?"

The three animals explained how they had first encountered Scar and the events that had led them to that fateful moment on the bridge.

"Well!" exclaimed the bull upon hearing their tale,"If what you tell me is true, I think we did the animal kingdom a great service today by getting rid of him."

The bull was also very curious as to why a goat, a sheep and a pig should be travelling together.

"We're on our way to the sea," Nelly pointed out. With all the trauma of the past few days no-one had even bothered to mention their original destination, or even think about it.

"Good idea!" nodded the bull, "I might pop down there myself later on with the herd. It might cheer old Daisy up a bit. She's partial to a bit of seaweed."

Upon hearing this, the three animals stared at the bull in amazement, stunned into silence.

"What's wrong?" enquired the bull, seeing their expressions. "What have I said?" Cuddles was the first to regain his powers of speech.

"Do you mean that we are actually near the sea?"

"Of course. Can't you smell the sea air?" Indeed, as he spoke the three animals noticed that the air was different: it was fresher, cleaner, almost newborn, with the taste of salt upon the breeze. They had failed to notice the change before, being preoccupied with the events of the past few days.

"How far away is it?" asked a very excited Nelly.

"No more than a mile, if you follow the river that is; shorter, if you cut across the fields."

"Which way? Which way?" demanded Gloucester, who had lost all self-control and was now jumping up and down in excitement. The bull pointed the way, whereupon Gloucester immediately charged off in the direction of the sea, only to be called back by the others who had not forgotten their manners.

"Go on, off you go," chuckled the bull, who could see that they were all very keen to reach their journey's end. "I'll see you later, with the rest of my herd."

The three companions bade him farewell for the time being, thanked him for his help, and raced off in the direction of the sea.

## CHAPTER EIGHT : AT LAST NELLY SEES THE SEA

The three animals ran up the gentle slope of a small hill and the cries of the seagulls could be clearly heard as they wheeled high above their heads. Nelly's heart was beating like a drum, in anticipation of what might be lying just over the other side. Then, as they reached the brow of the hill, they saw it: the sea. There they stood, silent, and gazed in awe at the vast blue expanse that lay before them, stretching out as far as the eye could see. Its sheer size and boundlessness, made it hard for the animals to take it all in. It appeared, to Nelly at least, to be so peaceful, and calm; its warm blue waters almost seemed to be sleeping, like a mighty giant at rest.

"Come on," cried Gloucester, as he charged off down the hill. "Let's take a closer look."

The others ran helter-skelter after him, across the field, through the rolling sand-dunes and onto the beach.

The feel of sand beneath their feet was a new sensation for all of them, having never even seen sand before, and each remarked to the other how strange it felt as their feet sank softly into the golden grains. Undeterred, they pressed on towards the shore line, a mere hundred yards ahead.

Nelly, who had outrun the others, reached the water's edge first. The thrill she felt was almost electric as she stood with her feet just in the surf and watched the waves break out at sea, while the water ebbed and flowed about her feet. She had made it!

Cuddles was soon to join her. He, however, was a little more adventurous than his friend and insisted on venturing out until the water had covered his knees, before appreciating their journey's end.

Gloucester, as usual, was last on the scene and, as always, went completely over the top, charging into the sea and wading out further than anyone else.

"Hey, look at me, you two," he squealed. By now he was

so far out only his head was visible above the water-line.

"You be careful," warned Nelly, knowing how accident prone he was.

"What's there to be careful about?" replied the overconfident pig. "What can possibly happen to me out here?" Unfortunately for Gloucester, his exchanges with Nelly meant that he was facing the shore line, and not out to sea; otherwise he would have seen the large wave which was heading towards him. Equally unfortunate for him, it broke directly on top of him. For a few moments he completely disappeared from sight, much to the concern of Nelly. Cuddles on the other hand wasn't quite so worried, knowing that it would take more than a mere wave to see off the world's most troublesome pig and correctly so, for a couple of seconds later he surfaced, coughing, spluttering, and beating a hasty retreat to the beach.

"If I were you, I'd stick to flying," commented Cuddles, as the distressed pig came splashing past him, heading for the safety of dry ground.

"It's not safe out there," he was quick to inform the others, who had found Gloucester's mishap rather amusing.

The next few hours were spent idly exploring the coastline, while Gloucester busied himself investigating the sand-dunes, which he considered far safer than the perils of the deep. This passed without incident, except when Gloucester received a painful pinch on the nose from an irritable crab.

By late afternoon the bull whom they had met on the bridge, as promised, brought his herd down to the beach. The cows picked at the seaweed which had been washed up on the beach, while the calves played and frolicked in the surf under the supervision of two matriarchal cows. The bull, whom they later learned to be called Oscar, introduced the three companions to the senior members of his herd, including the distraught Daisy who had lost her calf to the evil Scar.

Primrose, the most senior matriarch in the herd, and whose wisdom all respected, examined Nelly's ear and told her to bathe the injury in the sea, explaining that salt water was very good for open wounds and would prevent any infection setting in. She advised Nelly to repeat the treatment at least four times a day until the ear had completely healed. Such was the authority in the old cow's tone that Nelly had little choice but to comply with her wishes, and duly went off to do as she had been told. As is so often the case with those who have lived so long, the knowledge of a lifetime begets wisdom, and Nelly found Primrose's advice to be well founded: as the sea water washed over her ear, the pain eased and, for the first time in days, she felt some relief.

"Any better?" asked Primrose, upon Nelly's return.

"Much," replied Nelly, who had instantly taken to the kindly old cow.

"Now then," continued Primrose, "Oscar has told me all about your adventures, and of the part you played in destroying that wicked dog. But tell me, what plans do you have now that you have reached your goal?"

The three animals looked at each other. In all the time they had been together, the subject of what they were going to do after they had reached the sea had never been raised, and now that Primrose had brought the subject up, none of them had the faintest idea of what they were going to do next.

"To be honest, we hadn't given it much thought," admitted Nelly.

"Well, I think you ought to," stated Primrose, in a down-to-earth manner. "After all, summer's drawing to a close, and it will be winter before you know it, and I can assure you the beach is no place for an animal to spend the winter."

"I suppose we could always start to make our way back home," suggested Nelly, after a long pause.

"What! On foot!" protested Gloucester. "It would take months, and anyway, I need a rest. I'm quite worn out with all that's happened in the past few weeks."

"He's quite right," agreed Primrose. "It would indeed take months. In fact it would be winter before you reached halfway. You could easily find yourselves in serious difficulties, exposed in open countryside in some atrocious weather."

The heart of each animal sank as they realised what Primrose had said was quite true. They had to come to terms with the fact that they were, so to speak, between a rock and a hard place, with nowhere to go.

"No, there's nothing for it," declared Primrose, "you'll have to spend the winter with us."

"With you?" gasped Nelly.

"Yes, of course; and then when spring comes, you can all set off back to your own homes with the benefit of good weather ahead of you." Primrose's statement was made in such a way that it left little room for argument.

"That's very good of you," added a grateful Cuddles.

"Think nothing of it. Our home is your home. There is an old barn at the far end of the farm in which the farmer stores straw and where you can shelter when the weather gets bad, and there's always more than enough to eat. We're very lucky here. When the snow comes, the farmer always brings us lots of hay and corn; no-one goes hungry in the winter, so there's no problem there."

"Are there any oak trees on this farm?" asked Gloucester, hopefully.

"Quite a lot," Primrose informed Gloucester, "and you're more than welcome to all the acorns when they fall" she added, in anticipation of his next question.

"Oh good," was all Gloucester could say, as his face lit up into one of his familiar smiles.

When Oscar rejoined the party, Primrose told him of the plan to let the three companions stay with them during the winter. The news pleased the bull, who had grown very fond of the animals. The conversation then drifted onto general topics as the animals strolled along the beach, with Nelly and Primrose just ahead of Cuddles and Oscar.

"Your Primrose seems to have taken a shine to Nelly," observed Cuddles.

"Oh she would, you know. All girls together! Primrose is convinced that all males are born with half a brain: clumsy, awkward, lazy and totally unreliable."

"I know a pig who possesses all those qualities and a few more besides," joked Cuddles, before adding, "and while we're on the subject of Gloucester, where is he?"

The pig in question had decided to join the calves as they played in the surf, charging in and out of the water, squealing with delight.

"See what I mean?" Cuddles remarked to the bull as they observed his antics.

Oscar smiled, before asking, "But would you really want him to change?"

"Life would be a lot simpler if he was to grow up," came the swift reply.

"But duller! It strikes me that your Gloucester is, as you would say, an accident waiting to happen, but could you imagine what life would be like without the Gloucesters of this world. I dare say it would be a poorer place in which to live."

"I suppose so," conceded Cuddles, as he smiled affectionately towards the pig, who was making a complete fool of himself.

As the afternoon drew to a close, Oscar and Primrose gathered the herd together and proceeded to make their way back to the meadow where they usually spent the night, leaving the three companions alone to reflect on all that had happened to them over the past few weeks.

They sat down on the soft sand and watched the sun slowly sink into the sea like a giant ball of fire. Of all the sunsets, none are as spectacular as those at sea, and the beauty of such a spectacle was not wasted on the animals.

"Well was it all worth it?" Cuddles asked Nelly, as the last rays of sunlight disappeared beneath the horizon.

"Oh yes!" replied Nelly without hesitation as she gazed dreamily out to sea.

"A penny for your thoughts, old girl?" asked Gloucester.

"I was just wondering," began Nelly, with that faraway look in her eyes, "how far it is to the land of the palm trees?"

Cuddles and Gloucester exchanged glances, each perfectly aware of what Nelly was thinking.

"Oh no," pleaded Cuddles. "I think we've had enough excitement to last us all a lifetime."

"Definitely!" added Gloucester, in support of the sheep.

"Perhaps?" mused Nelly, who continued to gaze out to sea, with a mischievous smile on her face.